GHOS

Eva Figes was born in Berlin, ~~...........................~~ with her family just before the outbreak of the Second World War, and has lived there ever since. She graduated in English language and literature at London University and her first novel was published in 1966. In 1967 she won the Guardian Fiction Prize with her second novel, *Winter Journey*. She has also published four non-fiction books, including *Patriarchal Attitudes* in 1970, which proved to be a seminal book in the women's movement. Her novels include *Nelly's Version*, *Light*, *Waking* and *The Seven Ages*. Eva Figes is divorced and has a son and a daughter.

'A sustained lyrical monologue on the passing of time . . . *Ghosts* is a beautifully written prose poem, with the narrator's memories and thoughts vividly captured and measured out in paragraphs like stanzas. The novel is carefully structured and established in time and place.'

Times Literary Supplement

'In a rushing world, such a beautifully written, reflective book as this can focus our thoughts and doubts . . . Every reader must share this remembrance, be taken back with startling vividness to recall the compulsion . . . The rhythms of Eliot and Beckett resonate throughout . . . To have learnt from such masters involves a mastery, and Figes controls as few can the tone, balance and syntax of sentences and paragraphs. Her prose is rich and memorable.'

Country Life

'She sets about her haunting in a kind of spider's prose that sits and watches . . . When the moment comes to move it moves fast and straight. The haunting begins to bite . . . A novel of originality and distinction.'

NORMAN SHRAPNEL, *The Guardian*

Eva Figes

GHOSTS

FLAMINGO
Published by Fontana Paperbacks

First published in Great Britain
by Hamish Hamilton Ltd 1988

This Flamingo edition first published
in 1989 by Fontana Paperbacks

Flamingo is an imprint of
Fontana Paperbacks, part of
the Collins Publishing Group,
8 Grafton Street, London W1X 3LA

Printed and bound in Great Britain by
William Collins Sons & Co. Ltd, Glasgow

GHOSTS

First

1

Oh, my lost ones.

I thought I heard, I thought I was. No. This dark space.
Surfacing from: where? I thought I heard, I thought I felt.
Snuggling up to me, one on each side.

Yes. But no. Coming up from where, to here, what is this
dark space? I feel no one, nothing beside me. Only a dark
space. And my heart thumping.

Let me out, a voice cries from the dark space, from the
body which pants and sweats, heart thumping. This body
which is somehow not my body, tossing in the rumpled
sheets.

But now, silence. Only the clock ticking, and my heart
beating more quietly. Here I am. Once more. The steady
hum of the refrigerator coming through unlit spaces, the

eerie stillness of rooms at night. My rooms, yet somehow not my rooms. And the sound of rain on the window.

The sound of rain on the window, a dry pitter, and my heart thumping too hard. Let me out, I cry in the night, beating on the walls of this ribcage, my prison.

And yet, for a while, in the dark, I had them with me, light movements under the bedclothes, soft limbs gleaming out of the shadows. I had them here, alive, moving. No mistaking the turn of his head, her thick hair. No mistaking their quick living.

Which is real, coming up into this dark space as though drowning, heart thumping, a feeling of dread, or knowing their living presence, breathing, shadows like quicksilver, always on the move, but here? Or are both, and I live divided between sleeping and waking, and waking the nightmare?

No answer. My body which is not my body, sweating into the sheets. My life which is not my life, waking up round me, as the walls become faintly visible, what is laughingly called the here and now rises up like a prison, my prison walls.

The sound of rain on the window, a dry sound, and I struggle to go back under, under the dark wave, into the black ocean. For there I will find them, my lost ones, small and fragile, doing what they always used to do.

They used to come in my bed from night fears. Fear of the moon shining through the window would bring him. Thunder would bring them both, first him, then her, quite quickly, after the first rumble. Did it thunder? I heard nothing, only the sound of rain on the window, and my own heart thumping.

Rain pitters on the window, and the light is grey. Dull grey, growing paler. I am here, now. I was dreaming. No. Go back under. I was dreaming and the day is. Think. No. How did they look, in my dream? Could I conjure them back up, now, if I close my eyes?

I close my eyes and hear rain pitter on the window, the sound of wet tyres on tarmac, the swish and slush of water falling, traffic moving. I see, in the shadows, the turn of his head, her thick dark hair. But just what were they doing, and can I make them continue?

No. Under my closed lids, in the shadows, I catch only the shadow of a shadow, something about small white limbs, moving quickly out of reach, back into the dark. My life flowing away, vanishing, water into earth.

It fades, and the light under the curtain grows stronger. Here and now, what is left of it, my life. And the room is empty. The living of it, the real part, retrieved only in sleep. Oh my lost ones, found and lost, found and lost, with each turning of the earth.

So I rise, heavily, limbs weary as earth, sodden with the life run into it, and draw back the curtains. Water trickles down the window pane, and the light is grey, dull grey.

The sound is a sound of wet tyres on tarmac, the river of traffic flowing inward, into the city, the swish and slush of it, rain in the air, water falling, a sound known before waking, between dreams and coming to consciousness, heard without listening, but heard even so. Meaning rain.

All the paraphernalia of getting them off to school in time during wet weather. The hunt for the lost gumboot, always about to be outgrown. Brightly coloured hoods, waterproof coats.

Drops of water fall from a grey sky on to grey houses, a

grey road. Leafless trees are grey. Dark grey figures hurry by down grey wet pavements, carrying black umbrellas. Cars crawl bumper to bumper in the morning rush. Who sits in those offices now, and what do they think of, staring out at the rain?

The same figures but not the same, hurrying to the underground station. The same rain falling, rising, to fall once more. Do human beings come and go in the same endless flow? I doubt it. And yet: one way of thinking.

Fill the kettle. Time my egg from when the water boils: two minutes, thirty seconds.

The trees are still bare. Rain turns to sleet as it falls, eddying in the wind. The old man comes down the steps of the house next door, as he does each morning, to walk his dog. The same dog but not the same, can't be, not after all these years. Must go for the same type and colour.

Water runs in the gutter. Old leaves. The kettle spouts steam, and the water in the pan has begun to boil. Take the egg out when the minute hand reaches five.

Down the steps on the other side of the road comes the

young woman who just moved in. What do you mean, just, must be two years at least, no, three, the girl was a baby then, and now she's walking, with her brother bundled up in the pushchair.

She has trouble getting down the steps, which are too steep for her short legs. She takes them sideways, one at a time, always putting the left leg first. Reminds me. Not the same child, no. Only reminds.

First taste of tea, ah, good, and my egg is ready. Uncracked, good. Funny how I lose count of time, was it really three years? Could be longer, but seems like nothing.

Not the same child, no. Only reminds. Not the same dog either, come to that. This one is called Flip and the one before had another name.

The egg just how I like it, the yolk thick but still runny.

Not the same child, no. Only reminds. Outside the window the same sleet, the same grey sky, even the same bleak spring perhaps. But from a distance, say, without my glasses on, I could have sworn. It's her, to the life. The baby too, must be the same age gap between them.

6

Trees still bare. There, where the blossom comes, to the left of the window, not a sign. Nothing but empty twigs, and a few dead leaves in the sodden flowerbeds, also empty. I move from room to room, watching rain fall from a grey sky, run down the windows.

The exposed time, the waiting time. Waiting for leaf and blossom, one more time. The same, but not the same.

Broken fences sagging, gnarled trunks, old amputations visible in the wrinkled bark, everything exposed now before the spring veiling, crumbling brickwork and rust flaking off pipes.

I write: the same grey sky, perhaps the same bleak spring. Almost. Earth at the back of the garden is dark with rain, the lawn waterlogged. There, where the pram stood with a cat-net over it, gleams a pool of water. The black and white cat slinks along the muddy border, still with those three white paws and the small white bib. No, could not possibly be the same cat, only looks similar.

I write: what was I doing last year? Or the year before, at this time? A blank. Nothing. But there where the pram stood with a cat-net over it, where the ground is water-logged, I see her scream, looking at the mud on her hands.

7

Always finicky about dirt.

What was I doing last year, or the year before? Nothing, no answer. But, where the cat slinks, I see him thrashing about in the bushes, looking for his ball. Always the hours spent, trying to find the lost ball.

A fine drizzle now, and the sky grows paler. Will it stop now, the rain? I should read over what I wrote last year, to find out what I was doing. Reflected light in the room. Hearing birdsong, I walk to the window. Down below a familiar blackbird picks and hops across the muddy lawn. A wood pigeon swoops from leafless branch to branch. There have always been wood pigeons in those trees, a pair of them, as long as I can recall. Must be a different pair though, I suppose.

I write: how long does a wood pigeon live? And if it is so alike as to be indistinguishable, does it matter? No answer: only the sound of rain. Only the black cat slinking on three white paws, the bare branch swaying under the weight of the grey birds, and there, where the pram stood, a pool of water.

Speak to me, wood pigeon. I need your voice.

Hearing chatter, I move to a front window, where steam comes from the kettle spout. Down below a line of children passes, small boys walking two by two. Their voices rise, shrill as sparrows, moving down the road in identical uniforms. This is how it is, how it sounds, when everything is happening to you the first time round.

Tea tastes the same, the last cup like the first. Something to be thankful for. I told myself I would clear out those shelves.

Steam on the window. He would stand on the stool, or kneel on it, writing sprawling letters with his forefinger. Or draw animals. I see him now, against the light from the window, stretching up. Something about the back of his neck, from birth. Touching it, always touching it, with fingers, mouth.

And afterwards water running down from the sprawling letters, the simplified cats, two circles, two points for ears, a curling line for the tail.

Steam turns to water, running in clear lines down the window. Oh my lost ones. This absence. Was it all a dream? I hear his voice, with a frog in it, something froglike about him, his little croak. And her shrill treble. How they would squabble, pushing each other off the stool.

Stop it, I would yell, banging my hand on the table. But always, always fearful. Of sharp edges, glass, windows of glass, or stools toppling over. Thinking it out, what could happen. Stitches, trying to stop the blood, and my own panic. Thinking about sharp edges, corners, pan handles sticking out.

How still it is, I can hear my own heart thumping. And their voices, what has become of their voices now? I hear silence, and far off the city going about its business. Steam gleams on the window.

Wipe the window clean, and look out at the world. The rain has stopped for a moment, and round drops of water hang on each bare branch, every twig. Clear light shines through them. The street below is empty.

O brave old world, I think, standing at the window, staring. And now, while I stand, staring at the familiar outlook which has been changed, so utterly, the sun breaks through grey cloud for a moment and turns the hanging drops to prisms. Gold flash the drops, and blue, and red. Till the sun fades behind cloud.

2

The light changes, grows darker now. More rain on the way. But still I must move. Have no wish to move. Check, as always, money, keys, and so forth, and shut the door behind. Bang.

Move cautiously down steps. The woman who moves cautiously down steps, unsure of her footing, has become, is becoming, my mother. She could do with a helping hand now, putting each foot forward, as I have seen her do, oh, dozens of times, leaning forward slightly, something tentative about her movements.

There is a slight vacuum between my head and my feet. When I look down my head seems to float, not much, very slightly, and the steps seem a long way off. The gap between my floating head and the falling ground becomes more marked each day, slightly more alarming. I have no sense of my body holding me upright, the spinal cord joining head to unsure legs. It is as though my body has begun to vanish into thin air. Perhaps you have begun to

11

vanish as the city around you has been doing. Melting into mist, dissolving into grey cloud. I see their thin outlines fading in space, hanging on by a shadow. The shadow is in my head, the image in my retina, impressed on cloud.

Water drops from the naked trees. Watch for uneven paving stones, the unexpected dips and cracks. Getting worse all the time, holes, uneven surfaces, somebody could land with a serious injury.

Stepping, stepping forward. Watch where you put your feet. Used to hop, skip and jump. Left foot meant luck, or a letter. Avoiding lines meant something, striding in a funny fashion, paces being the wrong length. But now, simply watch that you don't fall, catch your foot on an uneven paving stone and go sprawling.

Water drops from the naked trees, and the gutters gurgle. A small child walking on the low stone wall, such a familiar compulsion. I remember: walls I have walked, or held their hands when they began to wobble. Low walls are intended to be walked along, every child knows that. Why?

I recognise her, chubby form, thick hair spilling from under the woolly cap. Yes. No. The same, but not the same. Another woman is holding out her hand, with an expression of impatience. Hurry up, she says. Oh no, don't, whatever you do, don't hurry it up.

A few sharp crocuses in damp earth, yellow bursting out of bare wood where the forsythia has begun to flower. A late spring, surely, another late spring. Here where the wilderness was, the old house behind trees, windows boarded up afterwards, and the flowering blackthorn. Here, where the children would run, creep through the hole in the fence, come back sticky with willowherb, grubby from bits of old iron, wood. Here, where the wilderness was.

There, where the row of shops used to be, the road widens and the traffic roars. My head spins slightly, the world floats. Watch that you don't miss your footing and fall.

There, where the row of shops used to be, a curved terrace with the bank at the end, topped by a little baroque cupola. You couldn't miss it, driving back from town, a distinctive landmark.

There, where the row of shops used to be, with the distinctive dome at the end, is a huge billboard. Something about flying or drinking beer. I used to think, when I saw that cupola, a bit ridiculous of course, but I used to think,

13

nearly home. Small shops, they were, one of each kind.

Beyond the billboard floats a mirage of metal and glass, reflecting sky. How long has it been there, a day, two days? Who put it up, and for what earthly reason? I lose count of the years. How absurd it is, this flux.

The road is a river of metal and glass, slushing on the wet black tarmac, reflecting clouds. My head spins, feet float on unreality, and there is nothing between my spinning head and unsure feet. But too much noise thunders in my ears.

Here, where the row of shops used to be, the old woman leans against a lamp post, hunched forward. Her spine is always like that, bent almost double, as though from the weight of the six plastic bags round her feet, and yet I know they are only stuffed full of old newspapers and bits of rag. She has been walking the streets now, how long? Some memory in the crazed old mind makes her keep going, a gash of bright red lipstick smeared across her lined face.

Here, where the traffic roars, and the florist used to be. I can do nothing for her, bent almost double over her bags of rubbish, in the soiled grey suit, the ridiculous old hat,

14

which speaks of better days, an old-fashioned middle class. I tried once, on a bitterly cold day, when I saw she was close to collapse, but she just shook her head. And smiled.

Here where the florist stood. My family have kept this shop since before the First World War, she said, when I bought a tall glass jar in the closing down sale. It only cost me a few pence, and I thought I could put branches in it, beech leaves, catkins, that sort of thing.

The traffic roars and drops of rain begin to fall, soaking the billboard, blurring the mirage of metal and glass. Fly, says the billboard, though now the white paper is grey and soggy, but I know it says fly, something of the sort.

Beyond it the car park, full of wet metal, rubbish of various sorts. I thought it was supposed to be temporary, how many years ago would that have been? Must be ten years at least, when the notice first went up: temporary car park.

What did I do with the tall glass jar? Car tyres swish and slush in the rain, and no sign of a bus. I telephoned the police, after she shook her head and smiled, bent almost double, face to knees, snow catching in the veil of her crumpled hat, but they said to leave her alone, once they knew who I meant. Is she carrying a lot of plastic bags?

they asked. I thought she was about to collapse, but no, there she still is, day in, day out. I find her in shop doorways, at street corners, bent double, turning her head askew with the lipstick smile. How many years ago was that, when I first saw her on the point of collapse, with the snow falling on her? I lose count.

Rain drums on the bus shelter roof. I hear the swish and slush, in a grey world, of tyres on tarmac. Close by me grey-haired women, middle-aged or worse, with plastic hoods over their heads and shopping bags. What keeps them going, once they get so old? It takes me a moment to remember: I am one of them.

Having had this thought, I instantly deny it. Not true, no. Number of years has nothing to do with it. Catch me looking anything like that. The working class grow old as the rest of us do not, or not so obviously. Bad habits, hard work. Just look at their legs.

Pushing and shoving to get on the bus, I push with the rest of them. Two huge young men in strange clothes force their way on to the platform ahead of us, and I exchange disapproving glances with a white-haired woman wearing a plastic hood. Who are these people, ask our glances, with their funny looks and their weird hair styles?

But, looking out through the rain-blurred window, I see that the wet streets are full of such figures, young, brash, of both sexes. They stalk the pavements in boots, high heels, wearing black leather, and their cropped hair almost always rises to a peak in front. Where do they come from, these invaders from space? How is it that I have not noticed them until now, or not in such numbers?

Fear is suddenly uppermost. Time has done this. I do not recognise this world. I live on the margin of death.

And yet, with the bus now stuck in traffic, through the raindrops running slantwise down the window, I see a street I have travelled down, how many times? Through how many years? The same street but not the same. I used to work round this corner, was it, or the next, getting off the bus each morning, slim, fashion-conscious, eyeing clothes in the dress shops, eyeing her own reflection too.

Demolition, reconstruction. Most of the old façades have gone now, under the grey sky. Does she still walk, that girl, in her pointed black shoes and sheer stockings, so conscious of herself, going for the distinctive look? Spending her lunch hours window shopping, or meeting him in that old-fashioned restaurant which I see no more, but see still, at that particular corner, with its round tables

17

and Windsor chairs, curtains and tablecloths, a set menu for five shillings.

I see her still, so conscious of herself, peering through the window to see if he was there, sitting at a table. I see the street, the grey façade, all uniform in those days, as though, in some other dimension, dust molecules rearranged, it still co-exists in the here and now.

Demolition, reconstruction. Dust rising and falling. The same city, but subtly not the same. There where the bomb site was, where the church stood, streaked with soot. It seemed an old city then, grimy façades unevenly washed by the falling rain, grubby shops and offices almost dark inside, with staircases smelling of rot. Old men plying their trade, retail and wholesale, behind gloomy windows with signs spelt out across them. My city.

This is not my city. Is, and is not. A river of human beings rushes by, much as usual, under their spiked umbrellas, through the falling rain, but without memory. Blind to the bomb site, the dust rising and falling, to the city beyond the city. Seeing no other self, no other street. Knowing nothing but here, now.

How surely they stride, between the cliffs of concrete,

concrete and glass, something definite about them, as though secure, each in his or her own body, unaware of being ghosts even now, as the dust rises and falls, and the sky grows light.

3

Rinse out, he says, having said it so many times before, and into the white bowl of flowing water I spit blood. Bits of mercury, tooth, and blood.

A bit more of myself goes down the drain. The drill in my head is matched by the sound of a pneumatic drill beyond the window, where scaffolding rises, dark rainclouds pass. I hear a thunder of girders, the sound of buildings rising and falling.

Think about it, he says, and I notice how white his hair has become. My head is full of words, such as bridges, crowns, old crown and post. My head is full of old crowns, old plumbing in bad teeth. Is it worth it? thinks my head, but my face is quite numb, and when my lips move I do not know it.

Rain splashes down the window pane. What an awful spring, he sighs. I just want everything to stay as it is, I

20

think. And ask: is that so unreasonable? I mumble something with numb lips, intending to get out of this room and stay out, for as long as possible.

Reprieved, but not reprieved, I wipe my mouth and get out of the chair. Knowing I will be back, perhaps within days. He has grown stout under the white coat. The decision is mine, says his gesture, but he smiles, knowing it is not. Of course, one could always drop dead before further intervention is required, and that is, if not quite a comfort, something to be taken into account. I take everything into account in my endeavour to avoid pain.

Think about it, he says, as the nurse picks up my coat. He had two little boys, both now doing something scientific. Each time I come there is another nurse, as though every season brings its crop. The smooth skin, trim limbs under cotton overall. A face with no memory, she turns, has turned, calls the next patient through the intercom, without a thought, carefree in her space.

I glimpse her from the landing, through the open door, briskly handling sterilised metal probes, and then it is time to go, standing with my hand on the banister, looking down at the dark shaft of space, my right foot poised above the stair carpet, slightly loose under the old brass rods, it was always slightly loose, important to watch your footing.

Down below the door with the curved fanlight, light showing through its leaded glass.

Below the hall table, with its pamphlets, the pot full of pale yellow daffodils. I come down the familiar old staircase, where I held his hand, her hand, to prevent falling. Where I hold on to the banister to prevent myself from falling. I hear the bell ring, and down below the front door opens to let in a woman bringing two small children. They are ushered into the waiting room. I am ushered out.

Sudden light hurting my eyes as I come down the stone steps, between spiked iron railings. The paving stones are drying at the edges. Is it me back there in the waiting room, could it be them? No. The same, but not the same. Like separate landings of the same staircase, going round and round. Yet somehow connected.

After the rain, the air smells wonderful. Breathe in and walk.

I walk on the paving stones, one two, one two. The house-fronts have not changed, familiar railings and area steps. I hear sounds, the same sounds, as a taxi behind crawls to a halt, the motor idling, and a door slams shut. The girl with her sheer stockings and pointed black shoes walks on

22

the drying pavement, everything light, loose and hopeful, keeping pace.

She will trip along the pavement, smiling though her shoes pinch. Glance at her reflection in anything that reflects, conscious of her distinctive look. Light as a grey moth, no more than a shadow on shadow, I see how she knows her own grace, how she carries her hope lightly, pausing at the kerb by the pillar box, sleek hair loose, limbs easy, the ghost of a smile at her mouth.

I never quite lose her. Behind, in front, in the periphery of my vision, she keeps up with me. She skips, hums a little tune under her breath, and the housefronts, being familiar, not having changed, confirm her passing. And so she flits, light as a grey moth, no more than a shadow on shadow, in the periphery of my vision.

And so I walk, with my tired tread, my clumsy limbs, in a world of shadows, where shadow exists on shadow. Time past and present, and future too, no doubt, since now is already tenuous. I glance at my reflection in a shop window, and see how the particles, dancing in their vacuum, rising and falling, have for the moment ordered themselves.

The shadows multiply. They lurk in the texture of old

bricks, faced stone, and gloomy basements. Where someone used to practise his violin, hour after hour, where I broke my heel on the kerb, where servant girls in uniform walked dogs, took messages, where she eloped with her poet. Where I walk.

I think of it, this continuum, as I walk along the pavement, one two, one two, crossing the lines, crossing the road where traffic thunders. And we shall all be changed utterly, in the twinkling of an eye.

The air stinks of exhaust fumes, here, where the church still stands, neo-classical, looking for donors to keep it up. An amusement arcade for troops during the war, tea and buns in the crypt. Remember it on account of the huge columns of the portico, and the player piano inside. We shall all die in the stench, as the fumes rise and the lorries thunder. How can this go on?

I go on, crossing the road with caution, knowing my responses are not as they once were. So many places to look, I could go in an absent-minded split second. An absurd way to go, try to avoid the absurd. Beyond, the park lies waiting, empty green spaces, a chill surface of grey water, mirroring grey sky.

The park waits for the continuum, for the crowds to come, and the sun. Lovers in boats will glide by, and ranks of coloured tulips blaze in the borders. But now grey rain-clouds pass in the grey water, which shudders a moment, and is still. Grey on grey, shadow on shadow, diffuse light from behind thin cloud as the skin wrinkles and becomes smooth.

On the cold grey surface swim mallards with dark markings, waterfowl with various feathers in wings, rings round necks, and so forth. Occasionally they plunge, into their own reflections, reflected clouds, breaking the fluid mirror. Rings run outward, a hint of the underworld beckons. Nothing more.

The park waits for the continuum, for the old woman scattering crumbs to sparrows; for the child trying to feed ducks by the water's edge. The same ducks but not the same, quick, full of life, snatching and swimming around.

She would stand there, laughing, choosing her ducks carefully, no, not you, too greedy, you over there, holding the bread too long, and unable to throw far. Until larger birds waddled out of the water and began to threaten, whereupon she would back off, whimpering.

The park waits, its green spaces empty, under a cloudy sky. The bridge waits, crossing the grey water. But see, there, where the child is running, stumbling a bit in its blue leggings. It is, surely it is. No.

Grey water reflects a rain-filled sky. The toy boat shivers on the rippling surface and keels over. It stands in the wind and will not return. How I stood, we stood, watching it anxiously as it trembled and swung, right in the centre of the pond.

The pond is a ring of cement. Here I stood, watching the boat dither in the wind, told them, no, no, don't worry, just wait for a bit. As my father had told me. Or perhaps: you must run round to the far side. And after a while, sure enough, it would drift to the edge.

This empty space, where grey water reflects a cloudy sky. Where raindrops pock the cloudy mirror as the next shower starts, and I put up my umbrella. I see a young woman begin to run, pushchair by one hand, pulling a toddler by the other. The blue leggings stumble trying to keep up.

Drops of water darken the landscape, soak into gravel and grass. Rain drives through the empty spaces, the mirror shivers, wrinkling. A wooden hut saying BOATS FOR

26

HIRE stands shut, and beyond it the playground is empty. Swings, roundabouts, slide and seesaw catch the falling rain. Not a sound to be heard, only the rain's pitter.

I hear them run. I hear laughter, from the wet rhododendron bushes. The swing begins to swing, the roundabout turns, and the seesaw goes up in the air. Through the raindrops falling, the rattle of leaves, I hear their voices calling, as a branch creaks, old leaves scatter, as the clouds darken and the wind blows.

And then the sky becomes light, I hear birdsong in the empty trees, and think, as the wind blows, from which bare branch do they come, these whirling white petals? I watch the shapes as they blow down, small, no trace of colour, blackthorn perhaps? But the trees are still bare, and they vanish, without trace. I see a petal melt on my sleeve. Snow, only snow.

Footpaths wind through the empty spaces, round the grey lake. Between empty flowerbeds, there, where the roses will show, I see my aunt stroll with her fat black poodle. Why, at that particular point? In a grey coat, with flat shoes. Out of the mists, from some forgotten Sunday, she comes now, and will continue to come.

The park is empty. The world is empty, wet, windswept and shivering, but my aunt walks on the footpath, turns to call the dog, who is sniffing round a tree. Overweight, with a cigarette lit. She narrows her eyes against the smoke, and the lashes meet, the creases show.

Why here? Why now? Her tread sounds heavy, crossing the wooden bridge, echoes in the hollow space below. A fat woman, humour lines round her eyes, who had been pretty before I was born. So her tread sounds hollow crossing the wooden bridge. And then? Nothing, into the mist.

More, I think, surely there must be more. But there is nothing. An empty expanse of grass. Grey water reflecting an overcast sky. A keeper picking up bits of rubbish on a spiked stick. Water drips from the leafless branches.

The children have gone from the playground, which stands empty. Swings hang from their chains, motionless. The pond is drained, full of dead leaves, and the hut with the sign BOATS FOR HIRE is shut. Nothing comes back. It all comes back.

A sparrow hops across my path. On the far side of the lake

the willows are hung with a faint green haze, first sign of spring. Nothing comes back. The eye sees for a moment, the ear hears, but look, now it is gone.

4

It is beginning to rain. The pavements, so lately dried, are dark with the first fat drops of water. Nothing comes back. It hangs suspended on the empty air, but look, now it is gone. What the eye has seen for a moment, the ear has heard.

Structures of glass and metal rise in the air, reflecting rainclouds. Early daffodils blow in window boxes. What does the eye see, the ear hear? Atomic particles coming together for a second, to vanish as dust in the wind? Stone turns to dust, dust hangs on the air.

Even as I think, a pneumatic drill thrashes the atmosphere, so painfully loud that I hold my hands to my ears and walk more quickly. I see a pit of yellow mud, old pipes and wires, the nerves and guts of the city.

Layer upon layer it sinks, into the mud. Until nothing remains but a few petrified bits of wood, an old bark sunk in the mud perhaps, or the head of a Roman god in stone, blind-eyed.

I know this city, and do not know it.

The churchyard by the cricket ground is now a playground. Swings and roundabouts between evergreen shrubs and an occasional stone angel. Only a few headstones still stand under the dripping trees, along the crumbling brick wall.

I know this city, and do not know it.

Stone turns to dust, dust hangs in the air. Here, where the semi-detached villas stood, with peeling stucco and wrought iron balconies, in their overgrown gardens. Stone turns to dust, bone turns to mud, and the mud sinks deeper. The gutters are running with water, I hear them gurgling.

Behind me the drill throbs, pierces the air. Now I am swept on a river of sound, it rushes by as the traffic thunders, cars swish through the rain. It is too much for me, the din. I am swept downriver, helpless as the rest of them.

What do they do with the old bones when they dig them up? What do they do with us?

Clouds move overhead, shade upon shade of grey, in an unending cycle. The rooftops gleam dully, grey with rainfall and slate, and windows reflect moving cloud. Through new struts and girders I see sky.

But the rain has stopped. Only the sound of water dropping from leafless trees, singing in the gutter. Stillness, just for a moment, and a sweet odour of damp earth. Ahead of me a child is running. She jumps into a puddle with both feet. My heart turns.

How to put it? As though my heart stops for a second, or misses a beat. It feels as if it were leaping out of its cage, trying to, before turning topsy turvy. The wool mittens dangling on strings. The manner in which she bends her knees, so close to the ground as she is anyhow, to regard her rubber boots, the water splashing.

Just so, I think, nobody else, no one but she would bend down to study the splashes on her boots, the puddle rippling. How unique this particular motion.

But the child's mother stands several yards away, holding an empty pushchair. I see her face is absent, eyes brooding and dark, with misery, is it, of disappointed love, or just boredom? Probably both, I think, knowing the look, the background.

She is far too young, I think, to know what she is doing. Smiling foolishly at the child, the way the elderly do, I remember. She is too young, I think, to know anything, and if she ever does, she will be too old.

Now it is my turn to smile foolishly at infants.

From where she stands, with the pool of tedium, of pain perhaps, deep in her eyes, staring into space, there seems no end to it. She sees, if she sees anything, just another absurd elderly person smiling foolishly at the child, the way such persons so often do.

How absurd it is, the time scale of things. To know nothing at the time of knowing. Turn around, girl. I who was once like you.

I look at the woman with envy, is it? No, a sort of distant compassion. For I know you, girl, as you do not know me.

Old leaves run in the gutter, which makes a gurgling sound. The light has become stronger, though clouds still drift over rooftops. Soon this year's crop of leaves will begin to sprout. Nothing visible now, in a bleak spring such as this, but it only takes a few hours for the tight black swellings to burst, once it begins.

Once it begins everything changes within hours. It only takes a little warmth, a little sun. Once it has begun everything changes so fast. The birds know this, I can hear them sing now.

Ignoring utterly the time scale of things, knowing but not knowing, the woman stands with her hand on the empty pushchair, whilst the pain of longing, the pain of tedium, collects in her dark eyes. They grow large with aching. Is there no end to this, they ask? How long must I stand like this?

But in a few hours, if the sun shines, every tree will burst into leaf. The birds know this, even now, singing in the bare branches. I know this. How the magnolia at number thirty-four will, overnight, burst into waxy white flowers, its brief annual show.

To drop its waxy curling petals on the ground a few days

after. The magnolia knows, in its wood, its bare candelabra of branches.

And she knows too, in fact. Which is why she stands, a pool of longing in her eyes. Here I stand, she thinks, and life is passing me by. Perhaps it has already gone.

She knows how spring is coming, and nothing will change. How she will continue to trudge wearily uphill, pushing her charge. She knows about the first signs of grey in her hair, and how day follows day. She stands in the rainy streets of tedium, hoping for change.

She would like something to happen. And I do not mean for the bare trees to burst into leaf. This is the symptom, she thinks, of my underlying fever, my restlessness. Each spring, she thinks, I long for something to happen.

Suddenly, overnight, the cherry trees will begin to froth and foam, the world fill with colour, but my life stays much the same, she thinks. Monotonous, and my hair turns grey. She does not know she will dream of the days she stood like this with her child, and think, that was the moment, then I was happy.

Rain begins to fall. I find my door key. See how the air is punctured by raindrops. As I turn at the door I see clouds move above the rooftops.

The rooftops gleam dully, grey in returning light, clouds reflected in upper windows, which shine. Nothing is what it seems, water falling, shadow passing, ghosts rising in the mist.

Shapes come and go like thoughts, thoughts acquire form as suddenly. So he walks in the clothes of another, so she stands for a moment, poised at the kerb, with a familiar turn of the head, her hair twisted in a knot, till the air stands empty, and the space is void.

So it was, for a moment, and now is not.

Second

1

Behind me, the notes sound with a curious clarity, following me along the stone passage which leads from underground. The two violins, rising and falling, the same notes, in an ascending spiral, the two voices, dancing round each other, as they have always danced, rising and falling round each other, like calling to like, echo calling to echo.

I hear the sounds behind me, the double melody, as I have heard it and hear it. The notes sing on within me, continuing the upward spiral even though the two instruments are now beyond hearing. I hear them still, in the continuum, dancing their double helix, as I have heard them before and will again.

Such sounds are not as earthly noises. Different from the footsteps, the dull thud of heavy packages, the hollow voice of the loudspeaker under the high glass roof, the whining trolley, and the dry rattle of the departures board as all names vanish. Such sounds are to us of eternity, they run in the bloodstream, pulse as a lodestar should, are, if anything is, the music of the spheres. Transform the humblest instrument, or instrumentalist. Continue even as they fade. Somewhere.

And yet the station forecourt has its echoes too. How many times have I walked, stood, bought a newspaper to kill time, passed through this hollow cavern of sound, with the high glass roof above me? Stood in line for a ticket, glancing at my watch, studied the indicator, arrivals, mostly departures, names and times coming and going, flip they are gone, just an utter void. And the platform is suddenly empty.

Today there are holidaymakers with bulky suitcases, and blue sky is visible beyond the high glass roof. The long platforms curve slightly, to a point where roof and railway lines almost meet. Almost, but not quite. There the sun shines on the signal box, on old brick surfaces, and the air wavers above the hot rails.

A pigeon walks sedately across my path, secure in its own space. Sounds are hollow under the high roof, martial music, the coming and going. Stand here long enough, and who will not come and go? How many times have you stood, coming or going?

Figures cross and recross the forecourt. Here, by the newspaper kiosk, where I saw Jim for the last time, quite accidentally, having run into him by chance, he stands, and stands, and stands. He was buying a newspaper before catching his train, and wore a dark blue raincoat.

Nothing remarkable about it. He laughed, said something, we both laughed, as he lifted his overnight bag. What did he say? The familiar head, hair prematurely white, so often glimpsed in unfamiliar living rooms, now caught sight of between a porter's trolley and the kiosk.

Too early as usual, I stand under the departures board, waiting for my train to be shown. The forecourt is full of shadows, gathering under the high glass roof. They are caught here, like moths in the globe of a lamp, ghosts in a haunted house.

An invisible network, a cobweb, lines crossing and crossing, the spun web of time in this space, as voices echo in the hollow space, get lost in the high glass roof. Where birds still flutter in the girders.

I stood, waiting for him to come on the last train before midnight, the forecourt almost deserted, meagrely lit, the place unusually quiet except for a couple of porters shifting mailbags. He came in a sudden rush of unknown faces through the barrier, his face known.

Unknown figures cross and recross the empty spaces, stand with their bits of luggage, waiting for a train to show on the departures board. A pigeon walks sedately at crumb level, past a paper cup, under a bench.

I will ring you, he said, smiling broadly. This smile, this gaiety, was something new. He stood in his dark blue raincoat, and I realised I was only just getting to know him, after seeing him so often at dinner parties, in unfamiliar drawing rooms.

He was off to visit his parents. That was it. Elderly people who must have been devastated. But of course I never got to know them. He had asked me to dinner, a joyous affair. The first, I thought, of many such evenings. Or used to think.

The shadows gather under the high glass roof. Now I count such evenings on the fingers of one hand. Grey moths which flutter helplessly, turning to dust. I see and do not see them, in the periphery of my vision. How many times have you stood here, coming or going? Stood here, holding a child by each hand, or a child yourself? Stood here, heavy with baggage, tired, or high with expectation.

With a soft clatter, like metal leaves falling suddenly off a mechanical tree, the names on the departures board vanish, leaving a blank space. I stand here now, as I have stood before, in this echoing limbo, watching the board for the right sign, or watching the barrier for the known face.

Nothing has changed much, in the station. Steam has gone, but the high glass roof remains. The departures board works smoothly now, no need for the guard to stand underneath with his long stick. But the names that come up are the same, and the same ancient soot lingers in brickwork.

The high glass roof reverberates with distant journeys, past leavetakings, arrivals. Martial music, a jolly march tune. I remember the soldiers in clumsy boots, sailors swinging kitbags, taking up too many seats. Children with too many toys, which they kept dropping. I told you not to, no, I'm not going to carry it. Struggling with too much baggage, and a child by each hand. Or I, in the distant shadows, being led by the hand, hearing the world exploding. The two straps across my chest, gas-mask and satchel. The comings and goings.

Nothing has changed much, in the station. Only the comings and goings are not what they once were, or perhaps have completed themselves, like a cobweb spun through a lifetime, gathered under this high glass roof. Ghost figures come and go, linger, hoping for just one more encounter, past, present or future.

All things become thinner, I see through them. Through the shadows, to others beyond. What would I not give for a smile of recognition?

But now it is time to go through. I find a window seat, lift my case into the rack. I sit, staring through the smeared pane, an unread newspaper folded in my lap, a book lying on the seat beside me. I am more interested in looking out at the vacant tracks, at the high roof, the old brickwork which reminds me of a cathedral. The texture of what is lost.

This is an old carriage, with a small upper window which opens. I push it as far back as it will go, but the heat in the compartment is stifling. Once we begin to move the air will cool things, but now the stagnant air is baking. It smells of old dust caught in seat covers, trodden around the dark brown floor, illuminated in a shaft of sun which has somehow managed to break through.

My life, I think, spun out like a cobweb, tenuous with half-lost memories, of sights, and smells. And the train begins to move out from the platform, one more time, and one more time the rolling stock grunts and jerks and creaks. The station draws back once more.

Hot sun strikes the carriage, spills on my lap, blazes across the dusty floor. It shines on the texture of cloth, the loose folds of my dress, reveals the crisscross of tiny lines in the loose skin of my hand. Folds of skin round the knuckles, protruding veins. The hand which has become my mother's hand, I recognise it.

The city recedes, as I sit with my back to the engine. Beneath a cloudless blue sky I pick out warehouses, ancient redbrick tenements, even a church spire from the jumble, of old landmarks, new buildings. Tucked beneath the seat, out of sight under the loose dress, are my mother's legs. I do not see them, but they feel less and less like my own.

The train moves faster now, running with the sun. Streets and suburban houses hurtle past, receding to where I have come from, converging to vanishing point so quickly. The book lies on my lap, but I do not read it. My eyes are hungry for vision, for things glimpsed as they fly past.

Known, but not known. Having travelled this route before, so many times, and by car too, though that was long ago, there are points of recognition, and of mystery. That curve in the road, with open fields on one side, a row of houses on the other, I am sure of that curve in the road. The road sweeps under the railway bridge at this point. But other landmarks are less definite. The small lake surrounded by trees, was it there we stopped on a Sunday, when I was still at school? And if so, was it on another occasion we visited the other lake, with a wooden jetty and the shore quite treeless?

My life, I think, tenuous as a spider's web in the wind. And no one left who would know for sure.

The sounds of a child further up the compartment are beginning to get on my nerves. It has not stopped since we left the station, whining and grizzling by turns. Now it has begun to scream.

If only it would shut up, I think, the sun burning on my arm, my mother's calves swelling unseen under the seat, the loose summer dress. My nerves are not what they once were, I think, knowing my response to the tiresome child is no longer mine, not what it would have been once.

But the route is relentless, I know. And through the dusty window I see the pasture with the old bathtub by the hedge, and two horses put out to grass.

Green fields skim by, and copses in fresh leaf, bright under a clear blue sky. The same leaves, but not. The river runs, runs.

And the train slows, draws into the empty station. And my heart stops, seeing my father on the empty platform, there, at the far end where there is only empty air, the ticket collector and a flowerbed. There he stood, always eager, holding his arms out so my children could run into them.

Now I am walking the length of the empty platform, where I see and do not see him. Where my children do not run. And I walk down the length of the deserted platform, my ticket ready in my hand, to where the ticket collector stands, as he always stood, in the same old station building.

And one more time I walk out through the dark little station, to where two taxis wait under the chestnut trees, but no one else, and ride through the small streets where nothing much has changed, except a name here, a shopfront there, the odd cottage painted.

45

I ride through the narrow streets where one more time the trees are full of leaf, foliage so dense, so thick, it seems like a miracle. A high tide, houses are almost submerged by it, green, shimmering under the bright sun. On the horizon a great wave poised, woods on the brow of the hill.

Everything greener, it seems, than ever before, somehow far more lush than I remember it, last year, and the year before that. I see irony in this, though perhaps I should take comfort. When the taxi drops me at the gate I see that the privet hedges have sprouted wildly, head-high and more. From the road the house is almost invisible.

I hear the sound of the taxi fading down the curve of the lane. A moment of stillness. Leaves rush in a sudden breeze, murmuring, and the sound subsides. Insects hum in the overgrown grass, and the newly opened roses.

It creaks, as it always did, the gate, and slams shut behind me. No damage visible, I think, staring at the curtained windows, though the paint on the frames is beginning to blister and peel. I try to count back to the last time they were painted, five years, six? As usual, I am vague about years.

But the key turns in the lock as it always did, and I step

inside, into the uncanny silence. It hits me each time, even now. Come in, says a voice, as I enter the shadows, as I put my keys in the dark green bowl which stands, has always stood, on the hall table. We know you, say the walls, as I hear my footfalls echo eerily in the emptiness.

I begin to open doors, and draw back curtains. Hot summer light floods in, striking the faded furniture, worn wood and thin carpets. I know every scratch, each mark and stain.

Two dead flies lie on the kitchen window sill, and a window jams when I try to open it. I have to bang the frame with my fist before it will give. The air in the kitchen is stifling, worse than the other downstairs rooms, and it has an unpleasant smell, as though something edible had been forgotten in the store cupboard. The possibility of something worse crosses my mind, like dry rot, for instance. I have no notion what it might smell like, but I do know that houses cannot be left indefinitely.

Last year's calendar still hangs by the dresser, two bluetits sitting on a branch. As though time could be held suspended. As though they had gone off on holiday, having emptied the bread bin, wiped down the empty draining boards, and disconnected the refrigerator.

As though each room waited for their return. The chairs grouped round the fireplace, the reading lamp standing where it always stood, and the foot stool he liked to use. Indented, like the rest of the furniture, with so much sitting, years of use.

2

I had not intended to do any of this. I came here to make an end, or at least begin to make an end. But I found the pull was too strong for me.

Having opened all the windows, including the french windows on to the terrace, having got some air moving through the stuffy rooms, I ran the cold tap in the kitchen until the brown water turned clear, and filled the kettle. This time I had even brought a notepad, and a tape measure, determined to be businesslike about the whole procedure. But I postponed the moment, knowing it could wait. Just half an hour, I thought.

Tea, I thought, filling the kettle. An iced drink might have been more appropriate, but since the refrigerator had been disconnected there was no ice. In any case, I felt like tea, even though the sweat was trickling between my shoulder blades, even though my dress clung to my skin, and hair was sticking to the back of my neck. I have always enjoyed the ritual of making it, apart from its taste.

So I took my cup to the terrace, to the corner which is always shady now, as a sharp angle of shadow cuts across the ground from the house, and sat, looking out at the garden, as we used to sit, handing round plates with slices of cake, arguing, as likely as not.

So many, I think, as I sit quite solitary, looking out at the lush green garden, and I hear the sound of spoons in saucers, the crack of bat on ball, and voices rising and falling, high, low, shrill, childish, murmuring. So many, I think, if you count the comings and goings, visitors coming by on summer Sundays.

And now I sit here, quite solitary, looking out at the green lawn, the silent trees. The visitors have all departed. Kith and kin like a cobweb blown away. Who would have thought, I think, time had undone so much, and recall the sulking schoolgirl, gawky in her checked gingham, who wanted to read in her room when visitors arrived, aunts, uncles, distant cousins.

So many, I think, and all, at the time, taken for granted. Criticised when their backs were turned, about money, manners, marriage partner, or laughed at for a silly hat. Who would have thought, I think, watching the silver birch quiver under the hot sun, shimmer under the high blue sky, time could undo the ordinary so utterly. The silver birch has grown larger, and the lime is now huge. But the emptiness.

I put down the cup, carefully. How she prized her china, more than the people who used it. And the china is still here, a complete set, twelve of everything, stacked in the cupboard. I cannot decide whether I truly like the design, or if I am merely used to it. I think about this, remembering, as I gaze out at the overgrown lawn, full of daisies, how much this distinction would have meant to me once, how vital it was, concerning, as it did, identity.

I see that cinquefoil has overrun the rockery. That was always my particular job in the garden, weeding the rockery. The sulking schoolgirl sits, quite alone on the terrace, surrounded by growing trees, trying to hear the echo of lost voices, caught like a dry fly in an old cobweb. So much for identity, that proud standing apart. Now I am what I have known, that which I was used to.

I get out of the rickety old deck chair and pull at a few leaves of cinquefoil growing at the edge of the rockery. The roots of this stuff are very tough, and difficult to pull out. As usual, only a bit of creeper comes up in my hand. I find a longer shoot, and this time almost a yard comes away, including a hairy root. Encouraged, I step further down the rockery, more or less on all fours, and continue pulling at the creepers.

I work carefully round the clumps of aubrietia and alyssum, stepping downward from rock to rock, still more or less on all fours. I know I will have difficulty straightening up eventually, but the hunt is on. I know it is a futile exercise, that the cunning creeper will win in the long run, but the war between us is lifelong, and I am not ready to give it up.

A stone loosens under my foot and for a moment I am helpless, foolishly spreadeagled on the slope. When I do find a firm foothold I have difficulty in shifting my weight without hurting myself, a cushion of alyssum, or both. I am conscious of looking ridiculous, but after a moment I recover my equilibrium, and am richly rewarded by two yards of creeper which come up, unbroken, in my hand. Ha, I say out loud, in triumph.

My back is aching. Sweat trickles into my eyes as I bend down. Even as a child I tended to be obsessive, if I did something, I did it thoroughly. So now I find myself searching between rocks and plants for the smallest leaf or shoot of cinquefoil which might still be growing. I feel slightly cheated at seeing nothing.

I sit down, gasping, dabbing at sweat. Grass, trees, sky, everything is a burning blur, it hums with the buzz of insects, trills with the high calling of birds. I go indoors for a cool drink, wash my face and hands under the tap. I am conscious of postponing what I came here to do, but my skin burns and tingles, I feel it glowing.

I look out through the kitchen window, to where roses are dropping their petals on the footpath. I remember how, in the old days, my body would glow like this quite normally. And I would stand at the kitchen window, staring at the roses, only half seeing them, dreaming.

It is terrifying, I remember him saying, how fast it runs. How old was he then, how old was I? I see him, his hair greying, a middle-aged man pouring the six o'clock drinks, and know that he must have been rather younger than I am now. I hear him say it so often now, almost hourly.

And because the sight of the unkempt hedge would have annoyed him so much I go to the garage and begin work with the shears. They are stiff with disuse, and I need the stepladder to work my way along the top. This makes me unsure of myself, but I persist, chopping laboriously at the dark green shoots. I have to take frequent rests, sitting on the bottom step, because it is so hot. I tell myself that keeping the hedges trim will make a break-in less likely.

A man walks his dog down the lane, and nods politely, the way people do round here. But I do not know him. Most of the people who were here when I was a girl have left no trace. This is not real country, where people stay from one generation to the next. This is a place where people come to find a green space, to escape from the city.

And the green spaces have somehow won, I think, dumping the hedge cuttings on the compost heap next to the incinerator. Everything grows and grows. Things planted when they first bought the house have got out of hand. Branches have had to be hacked off by tree surgeons, to avoid damage to the roof. The row of tiny conifers had to be thinned out years ago. I remember the apple tree newly planted, no higher than my shoulder.

Bees hum and circle near the trellis, where overblown white roses drop their petals. The unkempt lawn burns, bright with buttercups and daisies. If the grass is not cut soon, I think, the mower will not be able to cope with it.

I know it was cutting the grass on a summer's day, in very hot weather, just like this, which was the death of him, directly, if not indirectly. Even so I go back to the garage and pull out the lawnmower.

I am not going to push myself too hard, I think, taking deep breaths, sweat running down the back of my neck. Watching a blackbird hop out from under the laurel bush, I see the leaves of the poplar shimmer in a sudden breath of wind. And anyhow, I do not have heart trouble.

Even so, and though I get pleasure from the sight of buttercups and daisies glowing out of the grass, have done so ever since childhood, I start a ruthless beheading. The motor throbs in the still air. Just one more time, one more time, I mutter. Wiping the sweat off my forehead.

I used to sit at my bedroom window, a book open on my lap, furious at the neatness, their sense of order. Mats on tables, a special tool for trimming the edge of the lawn. I would sit at the open window and think, if it were my house, dreaming of a wilderness, high grass with butterflies coming out of it, a tangle of creeper round windows. Everything just growing.

I see myself, glaring furiously from my window, watching him pace up and down with the mower, the grass flying. Listening resentfully as voices rose from the terrace below, the tinkling of teacups, the incredibly stupid chatter of adults.

And I see him, as I did not see him, bent over the handle of the mower, trying to catch his breath, clutching at his chest. Did he fall, before she managed to get him indoors? And what did she do until the ambulance came? All this before she telephoned me.

I lean my weight against the trunk of the apple tree. Its twisting branches stretch over my head. For years the children believed it had grown from their very own pip, dug into the earth with a trowel. I never thought about it then, that my life, so ordinary, should constitute their wonderland.

Half the lawn is now neatly cropped. The air is full of the delicious smell of cut grass. I breathe it in, start up the mower, and continue, destroying the stillness as I move forward. When it is done, finally, I tip the pile of grass cuttings on to the compost heap. Just one more time, I think, wiping the sweat from my forehead, taking deep breaths. Just one more time.

I go indoors for a glass of cold water, gulp it down, fill the glass a second time. Outside the shadows lengthen under the trees, half the lawn is now in shadow. I sit on the cropped grass, in sunlight, smelling its sweet odour. And then I lie back, as I used to lie, so that I am gazing straight up into a clear blue sky, which goes on and on, up and up, inducing a feeling of vertigo.

3

I should be used to it by now, but not so. My body is out of control, even if my mind stays cool. A tremor runs through it, from head to foot, and my chest is thudding. It is at its worst as I pay off the taxi and walk up the gravel path to the portico.

The fine weather continues, but here it is inappropriate somehow, almost mocking. Since the old grey building is full of shadows, those who have no part in such festivity. Blue sky overhead, birds singing, every branch leafy, butterflies dancing in the hot air.

I go through the double doors, enter the shadows. As usual, my arms are full of gifts.

I know my way to her room by now, just as I know what to expect. Or so, at least, I tell myself. But telling myself, as I hear my footfalls echo down the hollow corridor, does not help much. My body is out of control, it follows its own rhythm, a panic rhythm. My mind stays cool, regarding the machine with dismay.

Outside her door I stand for a moment, listen. I hear nothing. Taking a deep breath, I shift things so as to have a hand free to open the door, the bag of fruit, my flowers. I turn the handle and step over the threshold.

I want my face to say: look, here I am. I step over the threshold with an expression which I hope is somehow lit up to say: look, who is here. But I hold the bunch of delphiniums in such a way that they also demand to be looked at.

The bed is empty. She is propped up in the chair facing the door, and her pale eyes register nothing. I should expect this by now, but it unnerves me nevertheless.

The walls are painted a pale shade of ice blue, and the bed is too large for the small room. I have brought a few bits and pieces to put on the mantelpiece, the dressing table. The china birds from her bedroom at home, a few photographs. Nothing registers. They stand neglected, askew, at an angle.

Now I have brought delphiniums, to go in the white vase. But first I put everything down, sit beside her, and take her hands between mine. They feel uncommonly light, the skin dry. She turns her head slightly, looks at me without recognition, but the hands stay limp.

I cannot believe it is too late, even now, or that the damage is irreversible. I cannot believe she will not respond to her own flesh and blood. That, if those dry hands once stroked my child's flesh, they will not know it now.

I do not know what brought about the revulsion. As a child I did not know, waiting for those hands to touch me, fondle me blindly. Or her arms to come round me. As an adult I understood even less.

But at least, now, she does not draw back. I hold her hands in mine, and she does not draw back. I do not know if she has lost the will to do so, or if she lacks the ability. Perhaps, I think drily, it is simply that she does not know who I am. If she did, she would pull them away quickly enough.

I try to think of something to say, holding her lifeless hands between mine, stroking the slack skin with my thumb. I think about all the things I have wanted to say for a lifetime, even now the pressure is in my chest. Instead

I drop the hands in her hollow lap, and pick up the bunch of flowers in their wrapping paper.

Look, I say out loud, removing the paper to show her. Your favourites. Delphiniums, picked this morning. From your garden, which you love so much. We are on safe ground now. I know she loved the garden, always did. If I could have brought Gip to lick her hands and wag his tail in a frenzy, I would have brought him too. And all the other dogs she cherished so wholeheartedly.

I see her eyes flicker, the lids come down for a second. Her mouth twists slightly, no, nothing like a smile, it resembles a moue of disgust, if it has any meaning. I am told by the doctors to expect nothing. I have told myself to expect nothing, for years now.

All of which makes no difference, if I am honest with myself. Somewhere inside that frail body, somewhere behind those cold eyes, the stubborn jaw, lurks my mother, the real parent I have never known. I want to draw her out, trick her, even now, into leaving her hiding place.

I hold the long stems of delphiniums across her lap for a moment, and wonder, if perhaps, after all, I am being cruel, rather than kind. The blue flowers thrust themselves

61

so audaciously forward, multiplying as they go. You can be proud of those, I remark, and fill a vase at the washbasin.

It is, of course, some time since she tended the flower borders herself. I remember her, doubled over, in old gloves and a frayed straw hat, poking at the ground with fork and trowel. I want to tell her how hard I worked to tidy the garden, but I am saving it up. Even if she does not hear a word.

Today the window stands open, which changes the feel of the room. I hear birdsong, and leaves stirring lazily. Down below on the lawn sit frail figures, bent and motionless, marooned in an ocean of green. A sweet smell of cut grass and the heavier scent of roses waft into the room, superseding the usual smells, of stale flesh, urine, and antiseptic floor wash. Sometimes the curtains move slightly.

I put the vase of blue delphiniums where she cannot help but see them, if she sees anything. I know she takes in everything, whatever the doctor says. I know she is sitting in judgement, even now, with the pillow behind her half-bald head, and a tube leading to the bottle of urine under her chair. She is critical of the way I have arranged the long blue stems, she will watch to see if I wipe off the rim of water on the surface of the table. Something like fury will rise in her if I do not, or if I allow the tap of the washbasin to go on dripping.

She is, after all, still my mother. All my life she has been watching for me to do something wrong. Spill something, leave a door ajar. All my life I have been satisfying such expectations.

I sit down beside her, near the window, still undecided about what to tell her. Should I tell her about the garden, or about the house? I do not know if it makes any difference, what, if anything, I say. It has also occurred to me that she would rather not be told, not if it is something disturbing.

I chatter brightly about the garden, about cutting the hedge, mowing the grass, weeding the rockery. Everything grows so fast, I say. I am being a good girl, I am trying to say the right thing. I know how easy it is to say the wrong thing, which is anything she would rather not hear. Anything she would prefer not to know about has always made her furious, instantly.

Outside the window green trees shimmer in the heat. Swallows skim and dip through a milk blue sky, and figures sit dotted about the lawn, spaced out like statues, catching the light. A sense of futility comes over me.

All this growing, I think, this bursting into song, this wonderful green celebration. As though there were something to sing about. As though it was all happening for the very first time. The birds mock those white-haired figures sitting on the lawn, catching the sunlight in their wheelchairs. White butterflies hover in mid-air, taunting.

Everything grows so fast, I say, touching her hand. Who would have thought the apple tree: remember father bringing home the sapling? She stares at me, frowning slightly, as though searching for lost words, discarded images. I am trying to help her, I think. If only she could find the words, even now, which she could never find, never bring herself to utter.

I believe I would know, even now, although she could not utter them, if she had found the words I have waited a lifetime to hear. I would detect them somehow in her pupils, the blue irises, something would tell me. They would flutter like trapped moths behind a window. I would let them out for her, uttering them.

I have her hand between both mine. It lies like a captured bird, and I stroke it soothingly. Although it does not try to escape, I am not encouraged. It is too inert. So this is how it is, a small voice is saying, nothing to do but let go. If I could.

I continue to stroke her hand, mentioning her roses in bloom, though now past their best, and how high the privet hedge has grown. Anything to avoid the silence. And the garden is safer than the house. I cannot begin to speak about the house.

The door opens and a young nurse comes into the room, bringing tea. Oh how beautiful, she remarks, nodding her trim head above the tray in the direction of the delphiniums. From the garden, I say brightly, getting up to help her. Mother loves her flowers.

A charade is going on, I know this. I hear it in my own voice, feel it in the way the nurse catches my eye, but I am glad of a change of mood. We fuss about the tray, rearranging the furniture, making room for it. The helpless figure in the corner looks on, silent. I feel she would like us both to vanish.

By now I find the nurse's bright, patronising tone quite out of place. Nor do I wish to go on colluding with her, as I feel myself to be doing. My, what lovely flowers, she says once more. Adding: will you give her her tea? in a flat voice, matter of fact, as though my mother could only hear the other voice.

She is saying something about the weather. Such a glorious summer. She laughs. We don't get many like this. No, I say, we don't. We congratulate each other on our good fortune. She has been sunbathing on her day off. Of course, she adds, some of the old folk find it a bit trying. But we get as many of them out of doors as we can manage, if only for an hour or two. Your turn tomorrow, she says loudly, raising her head.

After the door has closed behind her I begin to pour the tea, putting a lot of milk in the feeding cup to cool it down. For myself, I pour it out dark and strong. I think about the nurse chatting, think about weather talk as a form of bonding. I am beginning to find the heat a bit trying, though I do not say so.

I put the feeding cup to her mouth, and she draws back, surprisingly, making a small grimace. It occurs to me, as I try to coax the spout between her lips, that I do not know whether the nurse was joking, when she made that last remark. It occurs to me that I never do know, when members of staff adopt that loud voice.

I put down the feeding cup with a sigh, and drink my own tea, before it gets cold. A wasp has flown through the open window, it hovers round the small dish of jam which comes with the bread and butter. The tea tastes stewed, slightly bitter. Mother used to make it like this, letting it stand for hours. It could not be too strong for her.

The wasp has settled on the jam, and is greedily exploring its dark stickiness. I swish the air several times, then carry the dish to the window. Eventually it flies off. Outside the shadows lengthen on the lawn, the colours of the roses deepen. Shed petals lie at the foot of the rosebushes, the colour of flame.

I pick up the feeding cup and utter coaxing words. When did I last do this? I think, and remember. I try to imagine her feeding me, the time before that, but nothing, nothing comes to mind. I have no memory of her touching, holding, not a hug or kiss.

It seems, as I watch her face in its old transparency, hold the cup for her to swallow, that it must be my own mind which is defective. Nothing else could account for it, when I recall the touch of a child's skin. And yet I know this is not so.

She pulls her head back, frowning, and a grunt rises from deep inside her. She looks at me now for the first time, really looks at me, her eyes sharp with hostility. Or so I think, wiping the dribble of milky tea from her chin.

Yes, I know, I say out loud, looking at her but speaking to myself as much as anything. It's not good. I get up and walk to the window, for something to do. Down below a nurse is pushing an elderly man across the lawn, towards the house. Most of the lawn is now engulfed in shadow, but at the far end trees shimmer in slanting light, their leaves touched with gold.

Two more wasps have flown in and are circling the delphiniums, to settle for a moment on one blossom, then another, and buzz on. The angry sound all but fills the room, a nagging, intermittent threat. I pick the paper in which the flowers were wrapped out of the wastepaper basket and begin to swish at them, rather ineffectually. It takes me quite a while to get them both out. Beyond the trees the blue sky grows deeper.

If only, I think, as I turn back into the shadowy room, and look at the frail figure sitting in her chair. But the thought has no ending, no rational conclusion.

Speak to me, I cry, but no sound comes from my mouth. I know it is not feasible, that the time has long gone when she might have heard me. And no such day or hour ever did come and go. She might have been born deaf and blind, a being within who was sealed off, unwilling to see or hear, afraid of touching.

68

She sits now, with the urine bottle under her chair, her shoulders bent. I can see the pink scalp through her sparse hair. Her head trembles slightly. Her void blue eyes look in the direction of the door. I could accept more easily that she does not know me, which is probably so, if she had known me. But she has not.

Touch me, I cry, but do not break the silence. And my skin aches for consolation, for what it has never known, my birthright. And I touch, for something to touch, the blue delphiniums rising out of the tall white vase. Having shifted the framed photographs on the mantelpiece, just slightly, I begin to rearrange the stems of blue flowers, light and dark.

4

The key fits in the lock, and I enter into the stillness. Doors open on to other doors, and each object stands where it has always stood, where my memory holds it.

I open windows, step on to the terrace. I see that cinquefoil has begun to invade the rockery. This time, I know, I have come to make an end. I have decided how to go about it. I have made telephone calls.

One more year, I think, seeing the shadows grow long at the far end of the lawn. In the kitchen I hear the sound of the refrigerator humming, and go through the cool recesses of the house for a cold drink.

One more year, I think, hearing the ice cubes clink, seeing how rapidly they shrink, cracking in the liquid. The hedge, I notice through the window, is beginning to look unruly.

I must make a start, I think, putting down the glass on the draining board, and walk blindly into the study, my father's old den. I did not know I was going to begin in this particular room. Perhaps I did so because it had been left untouched for so many years, and because I knew it would be the hardest to tackle.

I open a bureau drawer almost at random. Old bills, letters too, brochures for pension funds and holidays, stacks of dusty paper to be tipped out, hardly glanced at before being piled into the wastepaper basket. If I once start to look through them carefully I will get no further.

Dust in the edges of the drawers, and a few rusted paper clips. An old pen, a few pencil stubs. Into the wastepaper basket go old greetings cards, concert programmes. Under an old calendar I find a snapshot, a girl in tennis clothes, squinting slightly as she looks into the sun, into the lens. The definition is not good. It takes a moment for me to realise who I am looking at, that the girl is, or was, me.

I sit down on the floor, and the breath has gone out of me. I am slowing down now, which I had intended to avoid. I find my own handwriting, something I did years ago, for his birthday, something I had quite forgotten until now. To find it now. Oh father.

I sit on the floor, my hands grey with dust, and let time pass over me. My will has ebbed away, as I was afraid it would. I must throw my life out, with the rubbish. I must let it go.

I put the snapshot aside, on the seat of a chair, but the futility of the gesture is clear to me. Nobody now will hold the memory, who and when. Or cherish it. I sit on the far shore of an ocean which has dried up. Nothing to do but recall.

And I remember, oh how I remember, as golden sunlight slants across the window ledges, as deep shadows fall across the lawn. The dark ache in the hollow house, where each angle is more than a memory. Where I tread like a sleepwalker, seeing the shadows gather round the long dining room table, each individual, his or her due place in the scheme of things, coming to join in the ceremonies. Names which are now only sounds, lost faces, links of cobweb blown in the wind.

I have come to compile a list, not of names, remembered feast days, but of things which must be disposed of, bulky bits of furniture, things which have been used. But before I can do that the detritus of living must go. This I tell myself, carrying a bin full of rubbish through the house. I have no notion how I am going to dispose of so much, it seems to me an impossible task, when furniture is imbued with a patina of use, has its own indelible markings. But I can make a start by clearing out old paperwork.

I walk in the shadow of the house, and every sight and sound is familiar. The air through which I move, warm, flowing over my skin. The smell of grass, and the sweet rottenness of the compost heap. The texture of all things, brick and leaf and stone, is part of me, hair and skin and bone.

I tip the rubbish into the incinerator and set a match to it. Beyond the lawn trees burn in the afternoon sun, turning their leaves in the lightly moving air. The blue sky rises, high, high.

White paper curls and turns black, as smoke darkens the atmosphere. It catches in my nostrils, stings my eyes. Through it the summer scene wavers. Fire lives in the death of earth, I think.

The blue sky rises, rises. Far up in the clarity I see a new moon, poised like a pale sickle. Swallows swoop and dip through the atmosphere. The lawn is now in shadow, but the trees still catch the light, each leaf incandescent. Fire lives in the death of earth, I think, air in the death of fire.

Bits of dark grey ash drift skyward, lazily, catching in my hair, rising towards the roof. Through the dark wavering air, the smoky atmosphere, earth and sky lose their definition, turn murky, and dissolve.

If it could all dissolve now, unreality into unreality, flesh turning to fire and air, bones cracking to purity. If the spirit could waft upward, into the blue, forget-me-not, but promising forgetfulness, true blue clarity, pure and endless.

If the illusion were not an illusion, the colour blue itself, the cool clarity. Music of crystal spheres, and so forth. If there were no dark beyond the fire. And further fire.

Swallows loop through the sunlit air, swoop downward. Tongues of flame lick at the paper in the incinerator, turning it black. I see smoke rising from the roof of the crematorium, while flowers with messages line the footpath.

Fire lives in the death of air, air in the death of fire. The trees burn, turning to ash and air. Substance turns to shadow, shadows rising in smoke. The world wavers, darkens slowly, as the sun sinks in the sky.

I am left with stinging eyes, and the smell of ash in my hair. I am left with rising shadows, and a house that, during the long nights, creaks in its fixity. I am left with ghosts, visible in the gloom, as the jasmine shows white in the dusk and its heavy scent fills the air.

Shadow moves on shadow, and tall trees snuff out like candles. The garden has become a mystery, and overhead a few stars have begun to glimmer. I stand in the moment, which is like no other, hearing the sounds of night coming. Bats flit in the dimming air, far off in the dark trees an owl screeches. I hear myself breathing, as the trees seem to be breathing now, cool night air.

Third

1

In this part of the country all trees bend in one direction. You see them against the vast sky, leaning inland. Life, earthbound life, seems minimal.

The wind blows constantly from the sea, bringing a salt smell. Only the toughest forms of life can withstand it, the most tenacious roots, digging through to the rocky subsoil.

In this country I sleep uneasily, hearing the wind battering the walls of the house. In my dreams I follow the contours of land as it rises and falls, lanes twist between headlands, an earthy skin on hollow cheekbones. I ride a switchback of waves.

In this house I wake fitfully, hearing the window rattle, and uneven floorboards creak. Seeing a light under the door when I open my eyes in the shadows.

Her bedside lamp burns throughout the night, whether she is sleeping, or not. I hear the wind moan in the dark and know she sleeps fitfully. I wait for his tread on the landing, for the low murmur of voices, and the sound of the kitchen door below.

Wind shrieks in the eaves over my head. Below, a dustbin lid rattles. Sometimes I get up to make hot drinks, or fetch water from the kitchen. Go back to bed, she whispers, between coughs, lying in an aura of yellow light. Pillows are stacked round her, the table by her bed crammed with bottles and glasses. She tries on her old smile between fits of coughing, spitting phlegm into tissues. Soiled tissues lie everywhere, on the bed, under it.

When I finally go back to bed I lie wakeful, hearing the wind moan, the old sash rattle in its frame. Furniture and floorboards creak in the night as though still living, after long silences which go on and on, like death. I lie awake, waiting for the sound to come again, but hear only my own breath and the wind dying.

In the morning grey clouds move swiftly across the sky, and the walled garden is littered with twigs and broken branches. Outside the world is grey, devoid of colour; inside the rooms look shabby, a bit dusty.

In her room the lamp still burns, throwing a ring of yellow light, on the grey ceiling, the colourful bedspread. Her eyes look very dark in her wan face, and unnaturally large, as though the pupils had finally swallowed up the irises.

She wants to talk, it is the thing she most wants to do, but it presents the greatest difficulty. She winces, swallows liquid, brings up phlegm. At times I try lip-reading, and she begins to laugh at the pantomime.

When she laughs I am struck by something luminous, the old beauty utterly refined, lighting her features. The self-deprecating irony in the lift of an eyebrow seems to me heroic, or very nearly.

Outside the wind still blows, ripping the leaves off branches. Grey light falls on the surface of wood, showing scratch marks, dust, the tired grainy texture.

She says, lying, in a whisper, that I have not changed. I sit on the edge of her bed, her thin hand under mine, and look into her eyes, which are smiling. Her pleasure at seeing me is almost childlike, but she gets tired too soon. I tiptoe out of the room as she closes her eyes.

I hardly know this house, which was to have been a new beginning. How many years ago now? Too few for a new beginning, it seems to me. But then I am like that, stuck in my ways. I cannot imagine such an uprooting, not now.

I wander about the landings, of which there are a great many, or so it seems to me. The house strikes me as dark, and impractical, with too many nooks and corners. Not designed for dying. But then, it was bought for living.

There are too many stairs, half-landings, and bare floor-boards. I am afraid of slipping when I carry a tray to her room. Without a tray, I find myself holding the banister.

It is a strain for her to talk, and her voice cannot go above a whisper. The urge to communicate shows itself in her eyes, eyebrows, lips, in the movement of her hands. She wants to know what I have been doing, seeing, writing.

I tell her, conscious of what she does not ask, has never asked. I love her for the silences between us. I tell myself, looking into her eyes, the light in them, that everything has in fact been said, told, forgiven. If it were not so, her eyes would not shine the way they do. I would not be here, holding her thin hand in mine.

We find each other, eyebrows, lips and cheekbones, under the changed skin. We recognise each other, under the changed contours, that is what we mean in saying we have not changed. Nobody else can do this for us.

She is now dreadfully thin, and the rings she still likes to put on slip round her fingers, pulled by the weight of the large stones. Jasper, onyx, that kind of thing. But she has stopped painting her long nails, and the old nicotine stains have faded. Her face looks more youthful without the make-up she once used.

Sometimes I say, rest now, and she leans back gratefully, closing her eyes. I tiptoe out of the room, shut the door behind me, and go down the uncarpeted stairs to the kitchen. I wash up coffee cups, tip eggshells and cigarette stubs into the waste-bin, and stare out at the grey clouds moving so fast beyond the window.

I listen to the house creak, to the silence inside and out. A door slams, and his footfalls sound on the uncarpeted stairs. I begin to make fresh coffee as he comes through the door. We avoid looking directly at each other, and when our eyes do meet his seem troubled by grey clouds drifting through them.

He sits heavily on the other side of the kitchen table, lights a cigarette. I put down the clean ashtray, and the burnt-out match goes into it. He will wait, leaning on the table, while I put out clean cups, bring the coffee pot to the table. After several days I know my way round this unfamiliar kitchen. We fall into the old rhythm, find it again. It expresses something.

We discuss the prognosis in low voices. He pushes the ash round the ashtray, using the discarded match. I watch his fingers, then study the surface of the table, running my forefinger along the grain. Both of us are struck by a kind of immobility. We do not look at each other. The door is firmly shut. Beyond the window high clouds scud overhead. I see a tree leaning, the wind stripping its leaves.

The hours go by in a subdued, shadowy stillness. Each room has bowls full of seashells, stones, bits of flotsam the colour of old bones. The souvenirs of antique storms. There are vases of dried flowers on window ledges.

But there is not much to remind me of the past. I wonder what she does with her old snapshots. A different house, I thought, in an entirely different kind of country, how like her that is. Each turmoil, every crisis would somehow resolve itself in a new colour scheme, different furniture.

And, as the wind bangs a door shut in the stillness, as the window rattles, I hear the old storms, doors slamming, voices rising and falling.

It all seems odd now, curious, the recollection of those distant storms, now, with the house so subdued, shadowy, a shell to hold suffering.

Do you remember? she asks, and picks bits out of the past, odd, amusing, like the bits of twisted flotsam gathering dust on window ledges. I see the children playing games on a foreshore. I see, was it the three of us, opening a bottle of wine at the edge of a ploughed field?

Sometimes she writes whole sentences on bits of paper, while I wait, watching her face. Or she uses her expressive hands, the long fingers with their rings slipping, to make up for the missing voice. She makes a game of it, smiling. For a moment eyes and skin have a translucent quality, like sunlight through cloud suddenly passing over a field. Do you remember? she whispers, as though I need to be reminded.

But soon the pain darkens her face, as sunlight passes. She winces, begins to cough. I hand her glasses of water, boxes of tissues, waiting for the paroxysm to pass. I breathe in the sweet cloying smell which comes from her, and which is always in the room.

Rest now, I say, and the words are full of deceit. She nods, closes her eyes, but without being deceived. She has left me far behind.

2

The wind whips through my clothes, and I lean into it, inhaling its sharp tang. I take deep gulps of air, cold and salty. Leaves whirl skyward into the grey clouds. The wind presses everything I am wearing into my body, skin into bone.

Grit flies into one eye, and the world dissolves in liquid. I turn round while my eye waters painfully, the wind pushing from behind. I feel on the verge of helplessness as I blink, wiping the tears off.

Only a moment ago I thought: I feel free, with nothing but air blowing about me.

The wind pushes me inland, while I want to reach the edge. I turn round, clothes beating like a sail, and lean forward, keeping my head down. I need one hand to shield my eyes, the other to keep my skirt down. I could do with a third, I think, as I thrust myself forward. Strands of hair work loose from my headscarf and blow about, whipping across my eyes, obstructing vision. I feel free, I think, tucking the strands back in, but they work loose in a moment.

A few spots of rain hit my face and I think about turning back, glancing up at the grey clouds moving inland. But they are too high, not dark enough, and flying too fast, I think, so I keep on walking.

Moving into the wind, with the land falling away on either side of me, the hedgerows providing no protection, I feel free, but conscious of risk too. I am small in a big space, liable to fatigue in fields of energy shaped without me in mind, that will not necessarily let up.

I am aware of blind fields of force, which do not recognise me. What am I doing here anyhow? they might ask. But do not.

I feel free, I tell myself, sniffing the brisk sharp air, looking up at the open grey sky above my head. The clouds move, I move, and for now everything other is blown away. But I know that the body I inhabit will only take so much, can only go so far. Rocks, stones, even the leaning twisting trees, all are harder and more enduring. .

The stones have weight and mass, and agonised trees are rooted deep in the craggy soil.

I do not wish to think about the human world, about anything, or anybody. Least of all my own world, and its contingent concerns. I want the wind to blow it out of my head for now, for the wind to fill my lungs and nostrils. Only to feel the land falling away under my feet and become part of it, earth, air and water, for as long as my body will hold out.

It will not be for long, I realise, hearing my footfalls, one two, one two, and my heart thumping, one two, one two, with effort, breath pumping in and out. The sea sings in my eardrums, the shells of my ears tingling in the wind.

Leaves whirl up into the sky, spiralling, are caught in the dry hedgerows, rattling drily. Seed-carrying down still holds in thorns and ditches. But the fields, heavy with recent rain, look sodden and far too green, having sucked in moisture and colour, all of it, from earth and sky. As the grazing cows seem to have absorbed the passing cloud shadows on their black and white hides.

For the light moves rapidly, so the land behind me is suddenly dark, then light, then dark once more as the clouds pass inland, over a faltering sun. Long grass shimmers in the passing light. My skirt flaps like a loose sail as I turn to look at the land, the passing light, and turn and look and turn again, wisps of hair in my eyes and mouth, blood and wind pounding together.

Grey rooftops gleam and turn dull, a dark slate colour. Grass ripples like water, dark side, light side, as sun and shadow glide over it, wind runs through it. A ditch glints for a moment and turns murky. Several winged seedpods spin wildly from a high clump of sycamores. In their damp musty shade I find a brief lull. They hold the wind in their branches, as it struggles to escape.

And then, suddenly, the land comes to an abrupt end. At a turn in the road, the long heaving horizon, the sound of breakers seething on sand, the scum of white foam on the shore. I taste salt and hear gulls screaming.

Blown by the wind, I stumble over the uneven surface to a group of rocks far back from the surging waterline. Within seconds my skin feels briny, I taste salt on my mouth. My hair, blowing out from under my scarf, is tacky. There is sand in my shoes, on my hands, under my fingernails.

Gulls ride on the wind from the clifftop, shrieking a song of chaos. White-winged, grey-backed, they wheel in the sky above my head, legs dangling, beaks forward. Their cries seem to goad the turmoil, to rejoice in it.

I lean against the rough surface of rock, feeling it scratch my palms, dig into my pelvis. The wind is now pushing facial skin into my skull. I am conscious of bones protruding, of my eyeballs as vulnerable jellies. I peer through half-closed lids to stop them prickling, the grit from flying in.

Where, at the far end of the cove, a rock has fallen within living memory, not aeons ago, the cliff face still shows its wound, pale, gaping. It is possible to fit the bit back on, in my mind, if in no other way. But in no time at all the surface will darken, the contours change.

And the din of water is in my ears, thrashing the shore. White foam runs up the sand, sizzling into it, breaking it down. The weight of it heaving, crashing, disintegrating. Changing colour as it rises and falls, from murky ink-blue to glassy green, as the clouds move overhead, obscuring the sun, then suddenly, for a moment, revealing it.

I lean against the rock, feeling the rough grit in my skin.

I smell seaweed, limp rags of it in the sand. I want all thought, all memory to blow out of me in the wind. I open my arms wide to let the rags flutter, open my mouth to taste the wind. Let flesh blow off my bones, pick them clean. I want nothing but this.

I am part of wind and water, so I think. My bones are as brittle as rock, sea water pounds in my ears, and I am swept free, glad to be on the wind, on wind and in water, with nothing to hear but the waves thundering, nothing to see but an endless horizon, with no human being in sight.

No point of identity, only sky and sea both moving, only a fitful sun glinting through moving cloud to change the colour of all things, this heaving churning flying mass, turning now black, now blue, from sharp turquoise to sludge green. As the rock changes colour too, light chasing cloud shadows over the length of dull mud turned rapidly to gold, and back to inert mud.

I watch, willing myself into it, the self-destructive mass, taking its din in my ears. A grain of sand blown in my eye floods the world, so even the razor-sharp edge of the long curved horizon, where ocean meets water vapour, where things vanish, is blurred, dispersed, and vanishing. If I could become rock, fixed for a brief eternity, immersed by the tide, by day, by night, until the rock turned to salt, crumbled to grains of sand, became one with the swirling sea.

I want no memory, nothing human to mar things. If a tugboat were to appear on the horizon, if the sea should wash up items of human litter, it would ruin everything. The wind has blown off name and number, the poor shreds of biography.

I could be anywhere, any place, any time. The sea obeys no clocks, knows nothing of ownership, recognises no boundary. The ship that ploughs it leaves no furrow. I could be anything.

So I think, standing with my back to the hard rock, its rough edges digging into my skin. I hear my heart pounding in the crashing waves, my voice shriek with the wheeling gulls.

I see how they rise and fall on the wind, flirt with the elements. How they touch the water, rest on it, bellies white as the surf, but untouched by it. Part, but not a part, of the heaving, surging mass. I smell salt on the wind, taste it on my mouth, my eyes and ears and senses are filled with the surf rising, the wave falling, the seaweed churned and turned in the glassy water.

I have no name, I think. All the sandcastles have been washed away, the scraps from past picnics. I have no name, no age, no number. The words scrawled in wet sand have been smoothed out by the incoming, outgoing tide, as have footprints, and small sandpies. Playing children have blown away on the wind, their voices faint, infinitely distant.

And if the words scrawled with a stick on the damp foreshore, the castles constructed in sand, if all this has been swept away, try to think of it purely, like this.

But I am landlocked. I must turn back. It is time to go. Imprisoned in flesh and bone, bone and flesh tell me I must start to make my way back. Plough my way through the dry uneven sand. My stomach hurts, my mouth is dry, and memory begins to ache. The tide is going out.

3

Let's go outside, he says, pushing his chair back from the kitchen table. Adding, I need some air. The atmosphere in the kitchen is thick with smoke. We have been sitting down here all morning, as usual. The ashtray is full and coffee cups with brown rings mark the hours.

She is sleeping, and when she is asleep a sort of heavy stillness comes over the house. We move about as little as possible, and keep our voices low. Even though she could not possibly hear us, we speak in whispers.

The old kitchen table in a new room. I stack the dirty cups, seeing the knots in the wood. My finger goes round and round, following the markings. The mood is still conspiratorial, as we speak in whispers, even though such oblivion is all we could wish for her now.

The cigarette smoke is thick with past hours, old thoughts revived, haunting us now. Far from being lost, they speak from the mound of ash heaped in the ashtray, from the dark rings in the coffee cups, and begin, stilly, to sing.

We open the kitchen door. A sudden gust of fresh air blows in, sending a newspaper flying. The smoky atmosphere clears, and a dry onion skin begins to skitter across the earth-coloured floor. I watch a ball of dust rolling over and over in the draught and think, I must wash this floor. Before I go I must clean up generally, as much as possible. He notices nothing.

The wind smells of rain, the earth feels soft underfoot, giving under my shoes. She was trying so hard with the garden, he says, but there is no sign of it now. It is tidy, but barren. What grows has been growing for years. I don't understand a thing about it, he adds, treading a cigarette stub into the soft mud.

It takes years, I say, for something to say. You haven't been here long enough. Glancing round at the unpromising damp space, with the grey clouds scudding overhead and brown earth showing through the thin uneven grass. A few sombre evergreens, but not much more. And so we stand, my heels sinking into the soft mud, staring at swaying branches.

The wind blows our hair round our heads, wildly. His thick hair has lost its colour, and he has put on far too much weight.

I can see where she put up a new trellis along the grey stone wall, and a limp, almost leafless shoot dangles from it, blowing to and fro. A few bulbs, I think, before recalling how far away spring is, and give up the idea, unspoken. It hurts to think of it. I say nothing.

It is our ability to say nothing which binds us, as much as anything. I am conscious of this as we stand, looking at the damp earth between our feet, with the wind blustering between us. If time has done anything for us, it has done this.

And time has done nothing to his hands. I watch his hands as he fumbles in his jacket pocket for matches, as he cups them around the flame close to his mouth. I am held. I look away, up at the overcast sky, where grey clouds are moving.

Let's go into the orchard, he says, stooping under an overhanging branch, and I follow his stooping form under the tree, past the weather-pocked sundial with its worn face. The door in the wall has wooden slats and a rusty latch. It creaks on its hinges.

I do not know where, or when, but as the latch rises and falls, clicks back into place, I know I have known other doors, or the same door, creak on its hinges, lead through the old stone wall. I do not know where, or when, only the small resounding sound as it rises, clicks into place. A memory of doors opening into just such grassy enclosures, and closing as quickly.

I hear her voice, how many years ago? I lose count. Too few anyhow. I still hear her voice, the way it used to be, arch, ironic, a timbre of self-mockery as usual: my dear, we have an orchard. Spoken as the lifelong city dweller, used to nothing bigger than a window box. And acting out a part, as usual. Wife, mother, and now this: I could hear her voice putting a distance between the pronoun and the thing itself. She always did.

The grass has not been cut in the orchard. Within the grey stone walls it grows high, up to our knees in places, higher where cow parsnip and stray seeds of wild angelica have been blown over the wall and begun to sprout. Startled birds rise out of the long grass as we swish through it, lift in a thrashing of wings.

The sound of wings, of grass, is in my body. I have been here before, a small voice whispers, knowing the long feathered grass, still wet from rain, how drops soak into my skirt. I ache with the twisted trunks leaning down to us, knowing their old scars, their enduring stance. Something about the rough stone walls, about the high stirring grass, the way we are closed in with the sky, moving dizzily.

Following him through the long grass, under the stooping trees, I pause for a moment, glancing up at the sliding grey sky, at the stone walls shutting us in. The walls rise and fall with the uneven ground. I know these things, coming together, moving through space and time in unity. I hear the voice inside me.

He moves slowly through the long grass, stooping under a low branch. I follow, catching my hair in some tiny twigs, and he unravels it, carefully. Hold still, he mutters, pipe between clenched teeth, and begins, very slowly, to free my hair from the overhanging branch, with detached absorption, as though it was a puzzle.

I have seen him do things this way before, many times. Breathing slowly over knots, bits of cloth, drawings. The fabric of things commands his complete attention. The strands of my hair do so now. Remarkably, it has not turned grey. It always was silky.

I have been stooping too long. When my hair is finally free from the branch my body aches to stand upright, the length of my spine. I push back my shoulders, firmly.

We are out of the wind now. I hear it, shrieking far off, moaning, in the high swaying trees. But here, within the high stone walls, both we and the trees around us hold still, becalmed. I hear the whirr of an insect. I hear the grass under our feet, and my own breath.

And I recognise it, this stillness. I have been here before, breath held between branches, and leaves making tiny sounds. Whether it was other walls, a different door, or the same door under the same sky, holding back the wind, holding the hour-glass suspended.

He says something about the walls needing repair. And the trees are very old. I look around his domain, earth-bound. When I look up at the sky it begins to shift, I feel dizzy under the moving clouds.

Windfall apples lie in the long grass, attracting insects. I turn one over with my foot and the underside is black, soft and foul. We get a lot of fruit, he says, but it is not particularly good. He begins to rummage in an overhanging branch, pipe clenched in teeth, and pulls an apple off from

97

under a cluster of leaves.

He holds the apple deftly, almost gently, with the tips of his fingers, turning it over, to look for flaws. I watch his hands, youthful still, their delicacy at odds, more than ever now, with the burly figure. I try not to watch his hands, spellbound. Something other turns.

I try not to watch his hands. Ridiculous, I think, after so many years, as he flings the maggoty apple from him into the long grass. But as he reaches up for a second amongst the leaves, as the stalk snaps under his exploring fingers, something within turns.

Memory turns, this key to a disused door. I feel how the lock turns over with a dull thud. A subdued grunt comes from him, since its skin is without flaw. He holds it out to me, one eyebrow quizzically lifted. His eyebrows have become denser, like the rest of him. But his hands are unchanged, unchanging. When I shake my head he slips the fruit into his pocket. His jacket bulges, shapeless, like the rest of him.

So how are you? he asks, leaning against the trunk of a tree, and looks straight into me for the first time. Now I see that his eyes are also unchanged. Some kind of veil has been withdrawn. Oh, you know, I say vaguely, since this is not the reason for my visit. I keep busy.

I wish he would not look at me, since this is not, not the reason for my visit. Until now we have had the sickroom between us. The pain of it has hung in the air like smoke, veiling the atmosphere. It could be said, truly, that there was nothing but common concern between us.

What was between us was her suffering, nothing else. Just a black ocean of pain, its waves sweeping away all landmarks, footprints, memory itself. Time has been drowned, I thought, seeing us like this. And was thankful for it.

But now, in this space, with the walled sky around us, and a gathering of mute trees, the old complicity. I have been found, found out, in spite of everything. Ghost fruit, of a vanished season. Each season haunted by its former selves. Where does the seed come from, where does it belong?

Grey clouds skim above the walled space. Brief gusts of wind rattle the leaves. Unuttered words skitter, echoing old questions, unasked. Did she say nothing for my sake, to keep me by her, through our years of loving? Did it matter too much, or not enough, in the long run? Was she too foolish to form the question, or too wise to utter it?

These questions I ask, and cannot ask, not now. When I sit at her bedside, holding her thin hand, the ghostly words, unuttered, hover like grey moths round my mouth. Loving her, I think she is trying to free me. I accept, and continue with my burden.

It was a mistake to come here, he mutters, shifting his weight, staring moodily at his feet. It was never the place for her, he adds, fumbling in his pocket, the one without the apple, for matches. He glances up at me, lowers his head to strike a match.

He looks at me through the smoke, and in his troubled eyes I find my answer. No need for foolish compunction. He is asking for me to help him, and I can do so, through the old complicity, and only through it. I stand upright. I am found, not hiding. We are old anyhow, and it is absurd.

Moving out here was a mistake, he repeats, shaking his head. His eyes, looking at me, are utterly lost.

Because she never asked, and I never told. Although she never asked, and I never told. Because we are old anyhow, and it is absurd.

I hear insects hum in the long grass. She only did it because of me, he adds. She didn't want to come, you know. I knew this, and said nothing. Into the silence he says: perhaps this made her ill. His troubled eyes find mine. Oh no, I say quickly, don't even think it.

We stand, staring up at the grey sky through the thinning branches. This, I think, is, and is not, the purpose of my visit. I am glad of it.

Above our heads the leaves begin to rattle. We stand, watching the rain fall, under a tree. The sudden shower falls into the long grass, darkening the soil, pittering in the leaves, before the shifting sky grows light as suddenly, a soft luminosity hinting of a hidden sun. And as we walk through the grass, drops running into my shoes, the air is full of its sweet odour, and a scent of ripe apples.

4

I wish you could stay longer, she whispers. She looks at me, her eyes grown large and much darker with her face so thin. I hold her hand in both mine, sitting on the edge of the bed in my travel clothes.

I'll come back soon, I say, stroking the moist hand. Hearing the hollow words fall in the dark room, wishing, oh wishing I could call them back. I was going to add 'in the spring' but managed to stop in time. Conscious of my own treachery, I add lamely: I'll write. Telephone.

Her face lights up with amusement. Our telephone conversations are most unusual, now that she has no voice. I interpret for her, one for yes, two for no she clicks through the receiver. A type of dialogue requiring real insight, that of a medium or mindreader.

I feel the large ring press into my palm. As usual, the room is dark, a bit dusty, with her clutter. An echo of all her rooms. A thin grey light falling on the earthenware pots, the bowl of seashells. I inhale, trying not to, the sweetish cloying smell which comes from the bedclothes. Outside, the grey sky moves and wind rattles the pane.

Time to go, I say, trying to make light of it. I squeeze her hand, so the ring hurts us both, and lean forward to kiss her. The bedside clock ticks by her pillows.

I let go, walking towards the door. In my travelling clothes I clumsily skirt round high vases of dried flowers which cling to the cloth, snagging the texture. I almost topple the teasel flowers, rustling in their pot. My body feels too bulky, overclothed, old.

Standing at the door I turn round one more time to look at her, to find she is lying with her eyes shut. So soon, I think, feeling lost. I am left standing, foolishly, staring at the immense fatigue which has cut her off from me, so suddenly. I wonder if, and if so, what images she sees under her lids.

I go through the door with as little noise as possible, shutting it slowly and gently behind me. I find I am shaking from head to foot. I breathe in on the darkened landing, preparing for my descent.

Down below I hear him shutting doors, clinking keys. It is time to go. The front door is standing ajar, with the suitcase nearby. Step by slippery step, I make my way down the stairs a final time.

Outside, with the wind blowing, the trees near the house bending, he puts my case in the car boot and slams it shut. The world, I think, looking up one last time at the grey clouds scudding overhead, the world through which I am going is not the same world. Neither is the traveller.

It seems curiously empty, this world, with its high grey sky, and trees blown almost bare of leaf. It skims past the windscreen, bumps under us, passing, passing. I try to recognise landmarks, but nothing looks as though I had driven this way before. But then I had come from the other direction, and we had been talking throughout.

Now there is almost nothing to say, or no possibility of saying it. He drives with the force of habit, hardly pausing at crossroads, accelerating angrily. The land flows like water, colourless, drab. There are no people.

The trees stand taller now, upright. Forlorn grey houses break the monotony, but without comfort. Impossible to think that life continues in these spaces. I catch a glimpse of an empty washing line above a broken-down fence. I try to think of life continuing.

The land rises and falls like water. I speak, when I do speak, of tomorrow and the day after with a kind of disbelief. Each word hangs by itself in a vacuum. It has no consequence: comes from nowhere, goes nowhere.

Now and then, as he changes gear, adjusts the steering, we utter the same old phrases. So we are not utterly lost, in this vacuum. It is like putting out a hand in the night, to touch another hand, intended to comfort. But, as he changes gear, turns the steering wheel, I do not touch him.

The road is wider now, and signposts stand out, large and persistent. Already I feel the small nervous tremor which has to do with taking off, with imminent departure. We are running out of time. Now that the road is a two-lane river of asphalt, now that the signs are large and persistent, we have put behind us the terrible conjunction of knowing both what we were and have become.

Now that we crawl in a convoy of cars, bumper to bumper, words achieve a semblance of normality. I glance at my watch. He asks me, not for the first time, just when I am due to take off. He assures me that we will get there on time: not much further now.

The landscape is flat, ugly, like any other landscape. Large billboards, concrete lots, a bottling factory. We speak more easily now, reassuringly, promising. The words slip out, having found their inconsequential flow.

And both of us are occupied with the business of negotiating objects: parking, taking out my suitcase, shutting the boot, finding the correct door which opens of its own accord. Voices echo in cavernous spaces, mingle. So far, say the voices, so far and no further. Take leave.

So, this is it. Under the sign which says DEPARTURES, having disposed of luggage, acquired a boarding card, we stand in the echoing terminus, facing each other. So, we say, and do not say, looking at one another for perhaps the last time. So.

Our arms go round. We stand in the middle of the bustling concourse, our arms locked round each other. Like two bathers trapped on a rock with the tide swirling up. As though, for a moment, we could stop the rush. As though we are the rock.

We are the rock, I think, perhaps say, into the rough texture of cloth and old tobacco smells. So familiar, but transmuting. And then I am walking under the sign which spells DEPARTURES, looking back to see if he is looking, I find him, the thick grey hair, his hand rises among the milling figures, he is still standing, then turns. I turn.

I am moving forward, through a funnel. I see his hand rise, I see him begin to turn, become one with the milling crowd. As I move through a tunnel, am conveyed on a conveyor belt, become one with the moving crowd. Propelled forward, to the dull grey sky beyond the glass, and the machine waiting on the tarmac.

This is the moment of nothing, of nowhere. This is the moment, as the wind blows round me briefly, as I glance at the grey sky and grey tarmac, climbing the metal steps to the metal mouth, when I consider, briefly, the possibility of going to my death. And enter.

This is the moment of nothingness, of nowhere. I watch the limbo landscape of grey tarmac under a grey moving sky, the sheds and structures moving, beyond them lorries moving on the distant highway, until we trundle on to the runway, until, after the moment of lift, the sheds and cars and highways diminish, become part of a scheme, and slant alarmingly.

The world tips, rights itself, but is no longer the same world. Sight and sound, the tree against the skyline, root into soil, rock into surging water, elemental configurations which have only just begun to colour my dreams and define my waking hours, all slip away, no more than an abstract chart.

Now I am nothing, and ahead of me is nothing. The past recedes, the future does not come. I see a patchwork of green and brown, insects crawling on thin lines, small mirrors of water, glints of light, the world wheels, turns, the sea surface wrinkles, and we enter cloud.

The past becomes cloud, becomes air. I am nothing but cloud and air, have nothing but vapour to hold me up. And we rise, rise, leaving behind the shadow of wings running over field and furrow, the shadow of cloud which darkens the deepest water, the small ship making its laborious way.

We move in a grey cloud, its thin wisps turn dense, white, we move in a snowy landscape which stretches endlessly now, under a blue sky with the sun glinting on our wings. Just like heaven, I think, the heavenly kingdom of childhood.

For now I am nothing. I should be a disembodied spirit, but I eat and drink. The sun blazes overhead, the sky is blue. Nice weather, remarks my fellow passenger. It always is up here, I say, smiling at his lack of experience, the foolish remark.

The blue sky rises, rises. I glance at my watch. Not much longer. Already we are falling, falling. The white bank of cloud becomes a grey fog on entering, and the patchwork begins to emerge.

Fourth

1

We used to come here as children, she says, and begins to tell me things I cannot remember. This woman who sits beside me, resting, has memories we do not share. I find this curious, but it is, I suppose, no more remarkable than her appearance. She is large, and no longer really young.

I listen, astonished, to a past I cannot remember. Even though we lived it together. I look at her and know that her present life is unknown to me, but that the past too should not be really shared is disturbing. Autonomy begins at birth, I think. And laugh. You little devils, I say, hearing how they schemed behind my back.

Are you ready to go on? she asks, and takes my arm. Until recently she would not have taken me by the elbow, to help me up. This is a new phenomenon, and I am still not used to it. This person who rises unsteadily is not me. I feel I should say as much to anybody who might be looking.

It was a good place to come on a rainy day, I remark. Weekends and school holidays were such a problem, particularly if the weather was bad. Together we peer into a glass case, and our reflections peer back at us. Amazing, she mutters. We are both truly astonished at the craftman's ingenuity, patience and skill.

I wonder what they were used for, she says, taken aback at their sheer size. I don't think they were meant for use, I remark, or they would hardly have survived.

Objects spaced out behind glass, each in its own blank cube, untouchable. I look through the glass and walk on, to the next glass case. I hear my footsteps, our footfalls, echoing in the high hollow hall.

So what are we looking at, she asks, turning her head inquiringly at me. I recognise the mark of interrogation in her eyebrows. Even now it makes me smile.

Craftsmanship, I say. Conspicuous consumption. Things that are really used get worn out, thrown away. Nobody thinks about them. We gaze at an ornate pitcher of silver gilt, with two matching platters.

All the same, she says, her nose almost touching the glass, I wouldn't mind having that. The lust for beautiful things is still strong in her, though common sense is her ruling star.

We turn into another gallery, badly lit, almost dark. This is not as I remember it from my childhood, I say, as we look through glass at old furniture, carved wood and fraying damask. Even the building has changed. I am trying to put back the building I remember, like an old jigsaw with half the pieces missing.

You've got a chair like that, she says, pointing, a hint of triumph in her voice. Recognition brings a faint flush to her face. I remember, she begins, telling some childhood story that has to do with the chair. She has fallen off it, been reprimanded for soiling the seat, and so forth. I listen, astonished, to a past I cannot remember.

But I am touched by her vivid memory of my chair, how simple things open up to become unique, momentous. Although I can take no credit for it, I nevertheless do.

We move on, hearing our own footfalls, not quite in step. Every sound echoes in this building, grandiose in a style that is not ours. It has been patched up, added to, modernised, but is mostly in a state of neglect. We are used, I think, to living with buildings that are not ours, were never intended for the kind of people we are.

We peer at intricate designs gleaming under glass. Diamonds which tremble like dewdrops. Unfaded enamel, untarnished gold. Pearls with their pristine bloom looking newborn, an everlasting summer captured in emeralds, the royal blood of rubies. Everything shines, definite and hard.

The golden horde, I say, of invisible cities, as we go out of the gallery into the modern stairwell. I think of a brooch which I lost forty years ago on a footpath in the country. It had small seed pearls round a miniature and had come to me from my grandmother. We walked back down the footpath but could not find it, either in the sand or the long grass.

We move on, hearing our own footfalls, not quite in step. I lost the locket you gave me, she murmurs, taking me by the elbow. I did not dare tell you before. It went back four generations, possibly five, I am vague about it now, how many grandmothers wore it in childhood.

I guessed, I say, ages ago. You won't be able to pass it on. I think of things found in sand, under rubble, buried. I prefer to think of these little heirlooms as buried indefinitely. But I know her house was broken into some time ago. She says nothing.

I remember, I say, there used to be a gallery, and we find it, almost as I remember it, if not quite. Old costumes set against tableaux of period furniture, brightly lit stage settings. Each dress, every jacket and hose stands framed in the right drapes, the correct chairs for the period. Nothing is out of place.

The gallery we walk through is dark, to allow each tableau to stand out brightly. Each scene is quite separate from the next, in a ring of darkness. The costumes stand empty, in their own setting, with knick-knacks appropriate to the period. Nobody stands in a room not of their own style. There is nothing in the costumes anyhow.

We walk on, hearing our own footfalls, in a building which is not ours, but which has been modified for modern use. We gaze at the rooms, brightly lit, where no son is heir to his father's furniture, no child plays an old instrument.

We used to come here as children, she says, blinking slightly as we emerge into the light of the stairwell. Perhaps she has forgotten saying this before, but perhaps not. She

114

has passed the stage when she wants to forget her childhood some time ago.

I know, I say. Hearing her talk as we circle the stairwell I find, as I have found before, that her brightly lit images are my dark spaces, as often as not. It seems, I say, as though the two of you were always conspiring, hatching childish plots. It makes me feel like a tyrant.

Oh no, she says, you knew what was going on. I'm sure you did. Did I? I am no longer sure of anything. When I think about it I remember myself as, if anything, over-indulgent. Of course you were, she says, that's the point. So why the plots? I ask, knowing the answer. No son lives in his father's rooms, I think.

I think of the angle of vision, how it transforms. Rooms that are large contract, fearful darknesses which vanish at the touch of a switch. I think of a world where it is easier to see under a table than above it.

On the stairwell I walk cautiously, taking one step at a time, using the banister. I see my mother move, putting out a tentative foot. Her body stirs round me, it seems to have taken over. Trapped in my prison, I proceed with caution. Messages between head and foot are unreliable, vision blurs into vertigo, just slightly.

Still free, still agile, she walks quickly on ahead. The old oil paintings have been hung in a new gallery, in their heavy carved frames. They speak their own language. These are the trees and sky of an invisible landscape, the outskirts of an invisible city. The trees are his trees, rising like no other.

All of them, almost without exception, depict a rural landscape, the few square miles of ground I have been living in, walking through, all my life. But I would never have known it.

I see his trees and sky, and look into his landscape. Whether it was, at any time, in his time, like this, I do not know. Even the pigment could have changed beyond recognition. I am looking into his style, and perhaps his vision. Beyond this I know nothing.

Not one invisibility, but a whole host, vanishing into the air, tower on tower, cloud on cloud. As branch rises on branch, leaf falls on leaf, his forest masses superimpose, vanish in a perspective of mist.

In close up, there are tiny cracks, like hairs, running across the surface. My daughter, who grew up within the same few square miles of ground, spent her youth here, is busy trying to identify particular spots. Is this the pond? she asks, steps back, and shakes her head. We go from picture to picture, discussing footpaths, clumps of trees, and both in relation to skylines. Nothing fits.

I give up, she says. It's not just the cart tracks, it's everything. Even the trees have changed shape. Or have been changed, I reply. Like memory, I add, this is composition. Like memory, vision turns to mythology.

She sighs, frowns, peers at a title carved into the wooden frame. The title is very specific. So is the museum's printed card, supplying dates. But I want to know, she says stubbornly. I recognise the look, the phrase too. I want to know, she would yell, argue, protest. Finding my child in her, I feel amused.

He is buried in the local churchyard, I say. Will that do for you? You can touch the headstone, it's solid enough.

She says something about being morbid. I would have argued about it, was about to do so, but she is suddenly somewhere else, vanished. I sit down abruptly, overcome

117

by fatigue. The effort of standing upright is too much.

Sitting down, each picture becomes an element in another picture. The pictures are hung, arranged. The room is cunningly lit, and leads to another room. Figures move, a young couple holding hands, a child running, a stout woman chattering to her companion. They drift through, obviously unsure, about how to look, and for how long.

I catch a glimpse of my daughter in the next room, just for a moment. I look at the stout woman, who is carrying too many things. I run my eyes quickly over the pictures, standing back, so to speak, to see how they shape up as pictures. I tell myself that I like the one in the corner best. It has to do with texture, and spatial relationships.

She comes towards me, in a body I no longer know, in clothes I am not familiar with. Each time I see her I am struck by this, the flesh which no longer seems to have come from me, which changes beyond my control, acts in a world I know little or nothing about.

As for what she is wearing, I have no idea how much is old, how much familiar to those who know her. There was a time when I knew the price and shape and colour of everything she owned. There was a time when the smell

118

of her skin was in my nostrils through the day and night.

Have you had enough? she asks, coming towards me. And I rise, feeling the fatigue rise with me, up the back of my legs through my spine, dragging my shoulders. Let's go, I say, taking a last look round the room, letting my eyes finish, and rest for a moment, on the picture in the corner.

In the corner by the door a moving needle writes, and having done so, moves on. As nearly as is possible, this is a controlled environment: humidity, temperature, light. Preserving pigment, trying to hold the vision, which cracks and darkens.

But I sweat suddenly inside my clothes, feeling my face burn, hands and feet prickling. We turn into the stairwell, the cool subdued light, and begin to spiral downward. She is ahead of me, moving fast in the grey light, the white light which turns to grey, and our footfalls echo, the sound rising.

She looks back for a moment and moves on, still going downward. I hold on to the handrail as the spiral begins to spin, and follow, step by cautious step. White light comes through the windows of frosted panes, rising as I go down.

When she looks back I see that there are dark shadows under her eyes, and that her skin has lost its first bloom. In this cold light it looks slightly muddy, with a blue tinge, reminding me of curdled milk.

I follow slowly down the stairwell, unsure of my footing. Is the foot below really mine? An enormous gap seems to be widening between head and foot. The foot hesitates, waiting for instructions, while the brain swims.

What has any of this to do with me, I think, foolishly, as though I was not here at all perhaps, and only a dizzy transparency remained behind. I am a ghost, a floating head, a disconnected foot, with nothing left to link them up.

We spiral downward, our footfalls echoing in the silence. At the last turning of the stairwell she stands and waits for me at ground level. We join the flood of figures coming and going. Passing through the shadows of the main hall, we lose each other amongst the crowd eddying round the exit.

2

White flakes fall out of a grey sky, which has been curiously dense all morning. For hours the light has been muted, leaden, a muffled stillness hanging in the atmosphere. Unmoving clouds almost touching the skyline.

Now the flakes have begun to fall, slowly descending in measured intervals, from nowhere to nothing. So it seems in the beginning, as they drift down, large, silent, to melt away on textures of cloth and stone, vanish in gleaming tarmac.

The spaces between them as they fall, drifting like frozen breath, are wide and clear. Between them, as they come down in feathery slow motion, out of the dirty fleece of sky, I see the spaces, the acuity, the clarity of brown and grey, the sudden solidity of brick, stone, concrete.

The flakes are large and loose, holding space within them, slowing their fall. They melt almost before touching down.

The black tarmac becomes glossy under the moving wheels, which change their sound, a sound still changing.

Infinity falls from above, measuring spaces, blotting them out. Insidious, soft as it falls, two falling where one melted a moment ago. Already the rooftops have become blurred, the two falling have joined with more, and slates stand out white, only outlines now dark.

The copper dome turns pale, green sheen fading to grey, its curve vanishing into misty grey cloud. The clock face has lost its markings, and the light its edge.

White flakes fall out of a dense grey sky, and leafless trees receive them. The dark twigs branch, holding out for oblivion. The air is filling with soft nothingness, multiplying to infinity.

It is clinging now to dark ridges of bark on tree trunks. To the rough surface of old brick walls. The sombre brickwork looks porous, as though crumbling away. The trees acquire a rigid immobility, devoid of leaf dreams.

As the air grows thick, blinding, the cars keep moving forward, their roofs now white. Wheels make slushy sounds on tarmac, and windscreen wipers swish to and fro. Eyes peer anxiously through the unexpected flurry.

Snow falls from above, measuring spaces, blotting them out. The billboard loses its outlines, what it depicts. The language of signs is silenced, muffled, rendered absurd. Windows lose their reflection, sound its echo. It keeps falling.

The bag woman leans her shoulder against a lamp post, and there is snow on her dirty shoulder. White crystals cling to the bit of veiling which comes down from her curious hat, and under the veiling her complexion is bluish, even the gash of bright lipstick across her mouth cannot burn off the cold. She wears what she always wears, winter and summer.

I try to think when I first saw her standing, with her shoulder up against a lamp post, and the bulging plastic bags round her feet. I know better now than to try and help her, as I did then. I do not remember how many years ago it was.

I do not know how long it is since she began her journey, round and round the same small circuit, leaning on lamp posts, pausing in shop doorways. I have lost count. Nor do I know whether I shall notice when she stops.

Now snow falls on the ridiculous hat, gathers on the rags which bind the bulging bags together, three for her left hand, three for her right. Her suit and hat were once stylish, I recognise the style. The gash of scarlet lipstick is as brave now as it was then, only the face has slipped, shrunk.

Only the cloth has grown soiled, the spine has curved, so her chin almost touches her knees. Only nobody wears those stylish suits now, or those ridiculous hats with bits of veiling. Nobody speaks the language they spoke, which had to do with breeding, gentility, expense.

Now snow falls on the ridiculous hat, on the bags stuffed full of old crumpled newspapers. Snow begins to gather in her hair, clings to her eyelashes, blinding her. Will I notice, the day she is not struggling along the road? How much time will have gone by before I miss her?

White flakes are still falling out of a dense and muted sky. The leafless trees receive them. Dark branches hold out for oblivion, turning white. Roofs are vanishing in a flurry of snow, blind windows rise on windows. The bench where the old man sat, year in, year out, with his walking stick between his emaciated legs, now has a covering of snow. IN MEMORIAM carved on the back is now illegible.

I forget the name carved across the backrest of the bench. I forget the name of the man who used to sit here. He had two names, the one he was born with, and the title he took to the upper house. Now I have lost them both.

Crystals of water vapour fall from the whirling sky, but each seems to dissolve, to merge, before I can see its shape, marvel at the infinite patterns. Footprints form on the pavement, showing up darkly, and fill.

Spaces of the privet hedge are thick with it. It gathers in the crevices of old brickwork. Blown suddenly upward, it whirls, descends once more, and catches in the slats of fences, angles of chicken wire fencing, the surface of signboards. FOR SALE signs become illegible.

It thickens on the roofs of cars, and mutes wheels in motion. The silence will grow, as it falls, until the world has no echo. Daylight is lustreless, almost grey. It comes to earth, falling like curling feathers.

It falls through space, defining it. Smooth grass plots

become pristine paper. As signs become illegible, a different writing waits. In snow I will read the passage of birds, in delicate hieroglyphs.

I will find the message of passing time in markings of blown ash, a shrivelled leaf, or water thawing for an hour.

Snow turns to water, water to mist. Each living thing turns into its ancestor. Who will read the passage of eternity, hour by hour? Snow turns to water, water to mist. During the night frosted ferns grow up the windows.

Hold the endless variations of this crystal if you can, before it melts, fuses. Catch it as it falls, before it turns to common snow. So water lives in the death of air, and earth in the death of water.

Snow falls on snow, wiping out imprints, how a squirrel scampered the length of the garden wall, and large black birds dislodged snow with their wings, hungrily searching. Forlorn stems in buried borders have grown heavy with cold bloom.

Footprints vanish. Markings of blown ash, bits of smut, disappear without trace, as do bare branches and bits of twig broken off by the wind. Fire lives in the death of earth, but it is black. Dead wood holds it, carbon, coal and ash.

But the child comes down the steps, cautiously, muffled up to the chin in a huge scarf, with a woolly cap on her head. She walks into a new world, tentative, unsure of this startling phenomenon. She puts her head back and sticks out her tongue.

The taste of snow will stay with her for ever. I know. Snow catches on her eyelashes, turning her blind, causing her to blink as the cold crystals make her cheeks tingle, she has never felt them tingle quite like this before. As though it burns, the snow.

She scoops it up with her mittens, which become soggy and wet. Crystals hang on the long hairs of the knitted wool and slowly turn to water. She can watch them doing it. I watch her as she stands in the snow, knowing every gesture.

Gulls wheel inland, snow wings under clouds of snow, from a forgotten sea. Their cries are muffled in dense falls, lost in a new oblivion. The horizon is annulled, distance wiped from the memory, as falling snow falls on snow, filling in footprints, vistas, every sign of order.

The child's mother comes down the steps, bringing the pushchair which holds the new baby. But the baby is no longer newborn, he sits up and takes notice. He swivels his head round to look at his sister, who is jumping about in the snow. Suddenly she is up to her knees in it, unable to move her feet, with the cold wet stuff sliding into her boots. She screams until her mother pulls her out.

Her mother is not amused. She pulls her out of the shallow drift, takes off her boots, first one, then the other, and shakes out the snow. I told you, she says, meaning she will not go back indoors to change her footwear. It has taken half the morning to get them this far, dressed for such weather.

I know the feel of the rubber boot under my hand, as I also know the sharp cold turning miserably wet. I know the betrayal, and the need to keep going. I know every turn in the cycle.

How long since the child in the pram began to sit up and take notice? How many mothers have come down those steps, how many children have grown quickly? Having never begun to count, I have no way of knowing.

128

Footprints are wiped from the memory as snow falls on snow, silently, relentless. Nothing is left in the visible world, closing in, but stillness. Only the gurgling cry of the wood pigeons, dislodging snow from branches. Memory holds the first taste of it on the tongue, how hands and feet would first tingle, then burn.

Drifts deepen where the abandoned house stands, its windows boarded up. It clings to the rough wood, collecting in the wire that surrounds the site. The glossy evergreens which have stood in this garden through season after season look darker, sturdier for it.

Until the men arrive with their machinery, in their boots. When walls fall crumbling, to rise in a cloud of dust. And the last remnants of ordered lives fly skyward, tumbling under the hammer, the iron ball. The evergreens will lose their corner, torn up by the roots.

Now silence and snow wrap the old house, hold it for the brief moment of drawing breath. For as long as it needs to hold the web of water suspended, to let it go. Until ice turns to water, memory to dust.

For the moment it finds a sort of celebration in dying. Caught in a web of frozen water, petrified mist, water vapour, a feathery dust of infinite variations, invisible, though always based on the same number, it is beautified by snow, its dark lintels and ledges, gables and crenellations stand out sharply, defined.

Snow falls on snow, blurring edges. The young man with the fair hair comes out to walk his dog as before. His hunched shoulders declare he will speak to nobody. He has been walking his dog like this for several years, so perhaps he is youngish, not young.

I have seen him walking his dog for so long now, several years. How many years is it? I lose count. Is it a year, or longer, since he found a woman, only to lose her within a year, or was it two? It seemed to happen so quickly, since I was told of her illness.

Now he walks as he did before, hardly visible in a flurry of blown snow, and speaks to nobody. It happened so quickly, from beginning to end. I would not have thought it possible, if I had not seen for myself. Seen the smile of greeting, faces changed suddenly by joy. Seen the wheel-chair, briefly, and the nurse arriving daily with her bag.

How long ago was that? I lose count, as I lose count of the

years, of the snow now falling out of space, defining it.

Feathery particles drop out of the dense sky. White sky, grey sky, a sky without echo. The city I have known is vanishing, bit by bit. Still trees hold out for oblivion.

Beyond the window, beyond the buried gardens, the dead trees, my invisible city joins all those that have gone before.

3

It gets dark so early now. By four o'clock the sky beyond the window is black, and the street lights are on. I draw the curtains and switch on the lamps. When the doorbell rings the room looks like a stage set, softly lit, every cushion sitting at the correct angle.

They fill the stillness with their words and voices, mingling. The hallway is full of their remarkable bulk as they take off overcoats, hats and scarves. I overhear them through the open kitchen door. I feel as though they have outgrown this space, brushing the walls with their shoulders.

I feel that I have shrunk. As they bent forward to kiss me, I was conscious of being reduced by their size, but their height alone could not account for it. No, as they grow I diminish.

The kettle begins to spout steam, and I fill the teapot.

132

Cups and saucers are already on the tray, so are the teaspoons with their curly initials. I have been using them for so long, I no longer think about the fact that the engraved initials are not mine, have never been mine.

My daughter comes, dutifully, to carry the tray. The cake, I say, is already on the table. And nobody takes sugar.

In the room, my son sits in my father's chair. He sits as my father would have sat, legs out, ankles crossed, wriggling his right foot. Sometimes I see only the way his foot twists, round and round. I see only resemblances, shadow on shadow, the ghosts in the living. My sense of the actual is changing.

At times I think I have no sense of the actual. Are things really here at all, I wonder, are any of us present? I think of my brain as a film negative that has been doubly, perhaps trebly, exposed.

My mother's candlesticks gleam on the sideboard. Pools of dim yellow light fall on my grandmother's rug. My walls look much as they always did, except that they could do with a coat of paint. After only, how many years is it, since the last upheaval?

I pour tea into cups and begin to hand them round. My daughter cuts slices of cake. Nobody uses damask tablecloths, she says, having glanced at the list lying on the table, not now. Think of the laundry, she adds, with a plate of cake in her hand. How big did you say they were?

For up to a dozen at table, I say, and most of them still in mint condition. In her day you had linen cupboards stacked for life. So what am I to do with them? I ask, remembering a wedding breakfast, the starched folds unfolding on Easter Sunday long ago.

My son's wife thinks they could do with a spare bed. Everyone agrees that the dining room table and chairs must be sold, since nobody has room for them. I mark the list accordingly. It's got a spare leaf that you put in the middle, I tell my daughter-in-law, such a commotion.

And see her leaning over the gap, tugging at the panel, with the french window open. And the sun shining. The window open and hidden birds singing in the trees. And everything still to come.

I see the starched folds unfolding, and she says: pull from your end. In a world where everything was still untouched, crisp and fresh as the cloth in my hands. I wore a yellow dress and the french windows stood open. Could that have been Easter Sunday?

I'd like the old nursery chair, says my daughter, apropos of nothing, and the painted chest. If you don't want them, she adds hastily, since they are not on the list we are studying. They are standing, as they have stood for years, in my spare room.

In the silence which follows I hear too much. My son is looking at her, but she is looking away, into the corner of the room. My son's wife is expecting a child in a few months, and if I had thought of giving such childhood furniture away, it should have been to him. So far I had not thought of it.

Oh, I say, into the awkward silence. My daughter's face is flushed, she sniffs suspiciously. My son's wife notices nothing of this, she wants to say something to him about the list, but his attention is elsewhere. He is looking at me, eyebrows lifted, in a mute question. What's all this about?

I know what this is about, now I think of it. In case I had thought of giving them away. So that he should not have something she did not. And something else.

135

The child in her, leaping out. Clinging to her childhood. Do you remember, she asks, remembering the painted chest, the old nursery chair. How we hid food in the bottom drawer? It went mouldy, she said, how cross I was when I found it? And I, who was cross, who found it, have no memory of it.

For a moment I have her, him too perhaps, I have a part in this drama, I am part of this drama which is being played out with much good-humoured laughter and even tears of sentiment. With a sort of disbelief I move centre stage for what seems a last curtain call, for a role I was not conscious of acting.

I laugh, hearing my own laughter mingling with theirs, seeing my own shadow suddenly loom large, a mythical figure of godlike proportions casting her shadow on to the ceiling, just a trick of the light of course. Only a childhood illusion.

Just for a moment I loom large, stand centre stage as I once did, before dwindling down, shrinking to normal size. Only my shadow plays in a world of shadows. I am clumsy with hands of clay.

Of course, I say, if you would like them, but nobody is

listening. The conversation has moved on, to a here and now of which I know nothing, from which I am excluded. I try not to hear, since everything I do hear shuts me out.

The words are of mutual friends I have not met, a mysterious common ground I cannot visit. I am conscious that somewhere, on a common ground I am not permitted to know, the party called life is being played out all over again.

I forget that I am tired of parties. I forget that I have met the friends they mention, and forgotten them. I am only conscious of being excluded. This is the first act of a new play, in which I am just the ghost.

I am a ghost on the periphery, watching. I am the child shut out. Overhearing, I want to join in. For now I am oblivious of the fact that it is not my turn. I have had my turn. It does not usually occur to me to live other than I do.

It is not that I hanker for lost youth. I do not feel I have lost it, that is the problem. I have to see myself through their eyes to comprehend, through their eyes I see the chasm. I think back to my former self in order to forgive.

137

That it is necessary to forgive, I think, standing up to go to the kitchen, is dreadful. I potter about in the kitchen, filling the teapot with hot water, unmissed, I think, hearing the voices rising and falling in the other room. My chest hurts slightly.

Beyond the window the shadows of leafless trees pattern the night sky. I see my own reflection in the glass, outlined against yellow light. Ghost houses loom out of the darkness, roofs and ledges marked out in snow.

Seeing my own reflection in the square of yellow light as I stand for a moment, looking out, hearing the sounds from the other room, I know how hard it is to be with them. I feel myself through their eyes, and become a creature I do not recognise. Do not wish to recognise.

I stand with the hurt, staring out at the night. Windows light up, distant figures move across the squares of light. Light years away, a frosty star winks above the web of branches. I find myself in the hurt, and that is something.

I find that I exist unscathed only in a vacuum, only in the long hours I spend by myself. And yet the wish to escape this vacuum, to make contact, is very strong. Too strong, I think, so my longing is bound for disappointment.

To make contact, I think, hearing the laughter come from the other room, watching the figures move across small squares of light on the far side of the dark road. To be touched as they used to touch, gladly, willingly. Not the dutiful peck on the cheek.

With the pot of fresh tea in one hand and a jug of milk in the other, I enter the room of voices and soft falling light. Rings of light fall on the white walls, across the piano, on to my son's hair, which has grown much darker. Nobody looks up as I re-enter the room.

My son, who is not my child, but who resembles him, sits in my father's chair. Sits as he would have sat, ankles crossed, wriggling his foot. I call him by the wrong name, something my mother used to do, and everybody laughs at my slip of the tongue. As I used to laugh, incredulously, when my mother did it.

I call him by the right name, handing him a fresh cup of tea. There is a dinner service, I say, trying to get the conversation back to the business in hand. It's rather beautiful, but I don't have room for it.

It is agreed that my daughter should have the dinner service, my son the glasses, for wine, champagne, sherry.

I go through the list, room by familiar room, dispersing it. From now on the shards of memory will come to me disconnected, in unfamiliar settings.

From now on there is no going back, except in dreams. I will pick up echoes here and there, in my daughter's kitchen, sitting in my son's living room, as my father's spirit speaks to me from the turn of his foot, the set of his shoulders.

I'm keeping my father's bureau, I say, looking down at the list, seeing his hand turn the key, seeing my handwriting amongst the rubbish of old bills, and hear my daughter say: that ugly old thing? I say nothing, seeing his hand turn the key, reach for his chequebook when I most needed it.

It can go on the landing, I say finally. I never have enough drawers to put things in. As for the stacks of photographs, I simply don't know where to begin. I nod in their direction as I hand my son's wife a second cup of tea, a stack of albums and boxes on the floor by the bookshelves.

My daughter leaps out of her chair, suddenly eager, and starts picking them up, the albums, the boxes. My son gets up too, and the carpet is strewn with snapshots, faces, more and more faces, young, old, babies with dummy features, looking wide-eyed.

I am called upon to recount history, a litany of names and relationships. I am aware of a world beyond their reach. I open a door on that invisible world, and allow them a glimpse of it. No, not a glimpse, something else. Only a story handed down.

Who? asks my daughter, and when? The further away, the more distant, the more clearly I remember the precise year. The summer I left school, about the time I met your father. Just after the war. I speak and speak, memory running out of my mouth so easily, a stream of living water.

And for a brief moment, in the warmth of the lamplight falling, I feel them by me, not as they once were, but as they are, flesh of my flesh, bone of my bone, in the warmth of shared memory strewn round us.

I hear my daughter say, do you remember? and laugh. You were always, I say, and laugh too. We sit round the circle of memory, and are the circle. My son says uncle, cricket bat, losing a ball in the bushes. You were always losing a ball in the bushes, I say laughing.

And for a brief moment I have forgotten the list on the table, I have forgotten how brief this moment is, this common bond, our blood pulsing in rhythm. Snapshots lie strewn in the falling lamplight. My grandmother's rug glows, the silver candlesticks from my mother's dining room glint. I laugh, but the hour of reckoning is upon us.

4

Snow glitters under the lamps, rings of ghostly light fall on the dark shadows of trees, houses. A crust of frosted snow gleams on branches, gateposts, the edges of footpaths. Overhead the dark sky is clear of clouds, and a few stars are visible.

I stand on the doorstep, looking up at the night sky. Living in this city, it is possible to be unaware of it, to shut it out of mind. So I stand for a moment, on my doorstep, breathing the cold air, looking up, up at the high dark sky, the black which is not just black, but holds blue within it.

The houses across the road are high and dark, their roofs of snow look ghostly, bluish under the night sky. Walls stand out black in the snow-filled gardens. Dark and light are reversed, a photographic negative.

Squares of yellow light up suddenly, here, there, coming and going. Black figures move across, so small, passing through the frames of light. Like an advent calendar, I think, each tiny box a lit stage suddenly revealed.

Counting off the magic nights, the magic hours, I think, standing under the night sky with its sprinkling of distant stars. Further up the hill the empty nursery school is strung with fairy lights, a lit tree stands in the window. The school is shut for the night, the children went home long ago, but their drawings hang in the windows.

I climb cautiously down the steps, taking my daughter's arm. The car stands waiting in the drive, its rear lights winking. My son, who used to walk up the steps of the nursery school, sits in the driver's seat. His wife sits in front, rubbing the windscreen and peering through it, my daughter and I get in the back. The back seat is full of rubbish which has to be pushed aside.

We sit in our shadowy box, in the dark, moving forward slowly. Ahead of us another vehicle, its rear lights glowing red. We move forward, stopping and starting, in a long line. There is silence now, in the car. My son, at the wheel, makes tapping noises with his left hand. A set of traffic lights ahead are firmly red.

I sit in the back seat looking out through the window.

144

Obscure figures with unknown faces hurry along the trampled snow, bluish light falling on them at eerie angles, heads down. Looking neither to right nor left, in a hurry.

The car moves with the traffic, flowing now, then stopping, starting. Dark cliffs of towers try to blot out the night sky, higher and higher. And they walk, the hurrying figures, through the ghost city, knowing or not knowing, as I do.

That this is a city without solidity. That since the dark cliffs keep rising, demolishing what was, the small, rendered precious with memory, is turned to dust, or if not, simply looks absurd.

Shadows fall on shadow, under the night sky. Garish lights blaze, lacing the dark façades, holding back the void. The inner city is a network of electric signs in the dark, but beyond the lights is a hollow city, under the high dark sky.

The car moves forward in the traffic, and nobody speaks. Suddenly I catch a glimpse of the dying moon hanging high above the rooftops, dumb as a ghost in the black sky, a forgotten relative. Even the name of the city is only an echo from the dark ages.

We move through the shadows, slowly, stopping and starting, as though in a dream. The dream holds us, but not quite. The signs beckon. This is it, they shout. But I look down a dark side street, figures hurry into the gloom, singly, each going into his own night.

We turn a corner and huge reindeer are strung across the sky. Every shop window glows into the surrounding dark, an Aladdin's cave of luxury and illusion. A discussion begins in the car, how it has no meaning, this festival of commerce. I say nothing, thinking, cavemen must have thought the winter solstice ruined by the new religion.

I sit in the back seat, seeing how the dark river of humanity flows past. We don't have much time, says my daughter, looking at her watch, as one more traffic light stands at red ahead of us.

Next year, says my son's wife, turning to him, putting her hand on his knee, we shall have a tree. I see her smile at him, the coloured lights catching her profile in the dark.

We leave the car in a dimly lit street, little more than an alley. There are traces of snow on old window ledges, area steps, and iron railings. The language of the past, I think,

146

seeing my breath hang in a fog on the dark air, each of us with a little cloud coming from us.

For a moment I stand in the dark alley, whilst my son is locking the car doors. Old brickwork rises to the night sky, and at the end of the narrow alley I see the bright lights, hear a hum of noise. I catch a glimpse of the reproachful, dying moon in the gap above my head.

The pavement is narrow, and we walk in single file between sooty brickwork and a line of parked cars. Into the here and now, cars moving, people pushing and shoving. Electric signs switch on and off, whirl in a garish kaleidoscope. Words spell themselves out, letter by letter, running the gamut of the here and now. This is it, they spell, shoddy, shifting, alive.

Above the street, against the night sky, Santa Claus sits behind his reindeer, huge, grotesque, his sack bulging with promises. Songs carol from doorways, stereophonic. The here and now is makeshift, transitory. The past is tarted up in a hurry.

But we reach the steps of the portico, which has not changed in living memory. Here I have been, here I came so long ago, sitting in the gods in my school uniform. We climb the shallow steps, through the stone columns, under the classical architrave, suggesting an ancient temple.

My heart beats now a little as it did, as hands flutter programmes, the face is found above the white shirt and bow tie, a fresh young face beginning to smile, him and her, her and him. Perfume and silk, gold rings and fur. But my heart is sluggish. The play, we know the play. But who is playing tonight?

The unmarked faces take up the old positions, ready to begin. Lovers meet tonight in the foyer, hold hands in the dark of the auditorium. We have found our places, studied the cast list to know who is playing tonight. The auditorium has not changed since I first came here.

The auditorium has not changed since I came here for the first time, so many years ago. Red plush, gilding, and chandeliers. It seems much smaller, that is all, slightly claustrophobic, the gilded moulding on the boxes, the high ceiling.

The lights go down, the curtain rises. I remember how my heart thumped the first time I saw the glowing scene revealed, sitting in the dark, in the gods. The words they speak are the words they spoke, time and time again.

148

Only the scenery has changed slightly, but not much. The costumes too, perhaps, but not much.

Our faces are lit by the wondrous lights from the stage. I see my son take his wife's hand in his as the play begins. I see tears in my daughter's eyes, shining in the dark as she follows the story. Behind the proscenium arch are a series of veils, diaphanous gauzes depicting in turn mist, twilight, the turn of the seasons, night and day. Each in turn rises, as scene follows nebulous scene.

Figures move in the lit spaces, speak words which others have spoken, touch hands and vanish. O brave new world, says the growing child, whilst the old man looks on, knowing how old it is. Youthful players speak words which others have spoken, as though for the first time.

Figures move in the lit spaces, not knowing how quickly the storm dies away, how often it has died before, and will, and will. They tread between gauze and gossamer, hearing music, seeing the sun rise, confronting the mystery. O brave new world, say the lovers, holding hands. We know the play by heart, if not the meaning.

How small it is, this auditorium. My back aches, I want to go home and sleep. Through the drowsiness I hear the familiar words, yet again. I am tired, so tired.

It is almost over. The scene has shifted, time and again. The curtain has lifted, and lifted. I have heard the audience clap as illusion followed illusion, each more insubstantial than the last. I have seen the old performer come to the front of the stage and remove his flowing white beard, showing a youthful face beneath as he takes his bow.

Wonderful, murmurs my daughter, feeling for her handkerchief. My son, glancing at his watch, and having seen several productions, is not so sure. I do not join in the discussion. I have nothing to say. I see only the door marked EXIT.

Eva Figes

The Seven Ages

'A bravely original book, a panorama of one thousand years of our history through a woman's eyes as uncannily moving as the birth and deaths that stud her poetic pages.

David Hughes, *Mail on Sunday*

'Bold and idiosyncratic . . . . written with evident passion.'

Penelope Lively, *Sunday Telegraph*

'Virginia Woolf would have so welcomed this book, representing as it does the direction she hoped literature would take. Here, at last, palpable, embodied, is that accumulation of centuries of unrecorded lives that she wished for. I read many of its pages in a daze of wonder.'

Tillie Olsen

Flamingo

Flamingo

Flamingo is a quality imprint publishing both fiction and non-fiction. Below are some recent titles.

Fiction

- [ ] CHANGES OF ADDRESS Lee Langley £3.95
- [ ] SHILOH & OTHER STORIES Bobbie Ann Mason £3.95
- [ ] BLACKPOOL VANISHES Richard Francis £3.95
- [ ] DREAMS OF SLEEP Josephine Humphreys £3.95
- [ ] THE ACCOMPANIST Nina Berberova £2.95
- [ ] SAD MOVIES Mark Linquist £3.95
- [ ] LITTLE RED ROOSTER Greg Matthews £3.95
- [ ] A PIECE OF MY HEART Richard Ford £3.95
- [ ] HER STORY Dan Jacobson £3.95
- [ ] WAR & PEACE IN MILTON KEYNES James Rogers £3.50
- [ ] PLATO PARK Carol Rumens £3.95
- [ ] GOING AFTER CACCIATO Tim O'Brien £3.95

Non-fiction

- [ ] CHINESE CHARACTERS Sarah Lloyd £3.95
- [ ] PLAYING FOR TIME Jeremy Lewis £3.95
- [ ] BEFORE THE OIL RAN OUT Ian Jack £3.95
- [ ] NATIVE STONES David Craig £3.95
- [ ] A WINTER'S TALE Fraser Harrison £3.50

You can buy Flamingo paperbacks at your local bookshop or newsagent. Or you can order them from Fontana Paperbacks, Cash Sales Department, Box 29, Douglas, Isle of Man. Please send a cheque, postal or money order (not currency) worth the purchase price plus 22p per book (or plus 22p per book if outside the UK).

NAME (Block letters) _____

ADDRESS_____

_____

_____